"Couldn't we at least exchange addresses?"

"I promise I won't make a nuisance of myself." Even as she spoke Roslin stole a glance at Tyson's face.

Impassive. Closed. Tense. She could guess what he was going to say before he said it.

"It's not a good idea," he replied heavily. "Let me be equally honest. We're attracted to each other, not much sense denying that. But you don't change lives on the basis of a passing sexual attraction, however intense. I suppose the smartest thing would be to go to bed with each other and get it out of our system—but for all kinds of reasons we're not going to do that."

"So," he concluded, "We'll do the next best thing—go our separate ways. Believe me, Roslin, it's for the best."

SANDRA FIELD, once a biology technician, now writes full time under the pen names of Jocelyn Haley and Jan MacLean. She lives with her son in Canada's Maritimes, which she often uses as a setting for her books. She loves the independent life-style she has as a writer. She's her own boss, sets her own hours, and increasingly there are travel opportunities.

Books by Sandra Field

HARLEQUIN PRESENTS
977—AN IDEAL MATCH
1034—SINGLE COMBAT
1120—LOVE IN A MIST
1242—RING OF GOLD

HARLEQUIN ROMANCE
2457—THE STORMS OF SPRING
2480—SIGHT OF A STRANGER
2577—THE TIDES OF SUMMER
1159—CHASE A RAINBOW
1178—THE RIGHT MAN

writing as Jan MacLean
2295—EARLY SUMMER
2348—WHITE FIRE
2547—ALL OUR TOMORROWS

writing as Jocelyn Haley
DREAM OF DARKNESS

HARLEQUIN SUPERROMANCE
88—CRY OF THE FALCON
122—SHADOWS IN THE SUN
217—A TIME TO LOVE
254—DRIVE THE NIGHT AWAY

SANDRA FIELD

goodbye forever

Harlequin Books

TORONTO • NEW YORK • LONDON
AMSTERDAM • PARIS • SYDNEY • HAMBURG
STOCKHOLM • ATHENS • TOKYO • MILAN

Harlequin Presents first edition July 1990
ISBN 0-373-11280-7

Original hardcover edition published in 1989
by Mills & Boon Limited

CHAPTER ONE

IT WAS raining. It was windy. It was dark. And she was starting to wonder if she was on the wrong road.

Roslin should have been wet, cold and frightened.

Although she was neither cold nor frightened, she was getting rather wet. The poncho that swathed her from head to knee had a number of seams which demonstrably were not waterproof, so that the cotton shirt she was wearing underneath was clinging damply to her shoulders. Her jeans, exposed from knee to ankle, were also wet, and her sneakers squelched richly with every step she took. Raindrops trickled down her face.

None of this seemed to matter. The wind that tugged at her hood and flattened the poncho against her body was a companion rather than a threat, its voice, which was rushing through the trees like the sound of the sea, the voice of freedom. She was free. As free as the wind. At this precise moment, no one in the whole world knew where she was.

Least of all Colby.

Roslin did a pirouette in the middle of the road, the poncho flapping madly so she looked like a truncated witch. Then, grinning idiotically to herself, she did a series of waltz steps to Strauss, singing the melody out loud, her arms embracing an imaginary partner. There was not a house in sight. She was alone in the world. Wonderful!

'Wonderful, wonderful Copenhagen,' she sang at the top of her lungs, dipping and swaying on the pavement. The less-than-rainproof poncho became a gown of white tulle adorned with sequins, and her partner, in dress-shirt and tails, had a tendency to look like Aloysha, whom she had met so briefly in Florence. Briefly because of Colby, she thought with a hideous grimace.

Then she nearly tripped, as the road abruptly changed from pavement to dirt. Waltzing became out of the question and Aloysha vanished, leaving her peering ahead into the rainswept night. The dirt road was pock-marked with pot-holes that were filled with muddy water. There was not a light to be seen. No signposts, no houses, no barns, no stray knights in armour charging to her rescue out of the darkness.

She had hitch-hiked from Boston to Maine; her last drive had been with an old farmer whose taciturnity had been excessive even for a New Englander. She had told him her destination, he had grunted, and that had been the extent of their conversation for nearly two hours. About an hour ago he had stopped in front of a dilapidated collection of farm buildings and waited for her to climb out, his craggy profile not bending an inch as she had thanked him politely for the ride.

She was beginning to think she should not have thanked him at all. The town of Carmel, her destination, had been described to her as a summer spa for the very, very rich. She did not think this road, slimy with mud and rough with gravel, led to the dwellings of the rich. But it must lead somewhere, she thought stoutly. Why have a road if it doesn't go anywhere? And, after all, what did it matter? She was free! She could walk all night if she had to. 'I'll walk through the wind...I'll walk through the rain,' she sang, with inward apologies to Julie Andrews. As she marched along the road, swinging her arms by her sides, she decided it had been a pity about Aloysha; she would have liked the chance to get to know him better. But Colby would not be around for the next man she met...

Ahead of her a glow of yellow light danced on the backdrop of black trees. Roslin stopped dead, and heard behind her the growl of an engine. Turning, she saw two headlights approaching, bouncing up and down as they encountered the pot-holes in the road. Shielding her eyes from the glare, she stepped to the side of the road. Her poncho was a dull green, and she had no desire to be sideswiped because she was invisible.

The vehicle, a grey camper, braked to a halt and the window on the driver's side rolled down. A voice said peremptorily, 'Get in—this is no night for walking.'

The voice was male, and it was telling her what to do. Under her breath Roslin counted to ten. Then she said, 'No, thank you.'

The man had obviously expected instant obedience. He said, 'Don't be silly—you're soaked. Get in!'

Roslin's eyes, hidden by the hood, were glittering, and Colby would have recognised the mutinous set of her jaw. But she said mildly enough, 'I don't want a drive, thanks. I'm fine as I am.'

'For pity's sake!' The man made a visible effort to control his impatience. 'OK, I understand, you're by yourself and I could be the Boston Strangler... I assure you I'm harmless to stray females, and I'm only interested in getting to the camp-ground and settling for the night. I presume that's where you're heading?'

In the reflected light from the dashboard, Roslin could see her would-be rescuer quite clearly. Certainly clearly enough to disagree with his claims to harmlessness. He reminded her of a sculpted bust she had seen in a museum in Italy, right down to the scowling brows, the aquiline nose, the pugnacious jut of jaw. One of the more successful of the early Roman generals, as she recalled. A queller of rebellions. A slave-driver. No doubt an executioner of helpless Christians. 'I prefer to walk,' she announced, and suited action to word.

His expletive was fortunately lost to the wind. He engaged the gears, drove a little ahead of her, and stopped again. 'I can show you identification, I don't carry a weapon, and I'm a respectable citizen.'

Roslin carried a weapon, an antique Italian dagger whose beauty in no way detracted from its deadliness, and she had refused as many drives as she had accepted in her journey from Boston. 'You may be all those things. But you don't know how to take no for an answer,' she observed haughtily. Just like Colby, she added to herself. Were all men like that? Intent on getting their own way, regardless of the wishes of the other person?

Her experience was too limited to tell. But she was not about to expand it with this particular man.

He grated, 'Are you or are you not going to the Penisquit Bay Camp-Ground?'

'I am not.'

'Then where are you going?'

Another policy on her flight from the city had been to keep her destination to herself. 'Buckton,' she said calmly, naming the town twenty miles beyond Carmel.

'You're on the wrong road. This road goes to the camp-ground and the fishing village of Penisquit, then ends in a farmer's field.'

She knew instantly that he was telling the truth. Cursing the old man who had put her in this predicament, Roslin said with great dignity, 'In that case, I'd better turn back. Thank you for the information.'

A sudden gust of wind belled the poncho about her waist, and a sheet of rain drove needles into her face. She ducked her head, staggering against the wind's force. It would be in her face all the way back, she realised with a sinking heart. Freedom did not seem quite the rousing battle cry it had been a few minutes ago.

The door of the van slammed. The man strode round the back of the van, grabbed her arm through the rubberised folds of the poncho and yelled, 'Don't be an idiot! You're miles out of your way, and the chances of getting a lift are just about nil. I'm going towards Buckton tomorrow, I'll put you on the right road at least. Get in the van!'

They were standing near the brake lights, which cast an unearthly red glow over the man's features, transforming him into a figure from the Inferno. Black eyes set in pits. Black hair writhing in the wind. Teeth white as bone. Roslin shook her arm free and yelled back, 'Stop telling me what to do!'

'There's not another house between here and the campground, and you're six miles from a village the other way. Do you honestly think I can leave you here in this kind of weather at ten o'clock at night and live with my conscience? What kind of person would that make me?'

'I don't care about your stupid conscience! I'm sick to death of being ordered around and I'm perfectly capable of walking six miles. It's only rain, for goodness' sake—it won't kill me!'

Another squall lashed at her face. She planted her feet in the mud, stood firm, and saw with no compunction whatsoever that the man's short-sleeved shirt was already plastered to his chest. Serve him right for interfering, she thought unkindly. 'You've done your Good Samaritan act for the day, and I absolve you of any blame,' she added. 'This particular traveller doesn't want rescuing.'

In the dim light she missed his sudden intention. He closed the distance between them, picked her up bodily, and lugged her, frozen with surprise, around the front of the camper. The glare of the headlights blinded her. Eyes squeezed shut, feeling like a Sabine woman in the throes of being abducted, she tried to kick him. He might look like a Roman general, but she was damned if she was going to let him behave like one. Again she lashed out with her feet.

She could have saved herself the trouble. The man was strong, and the poncho hampered her from getting any leverage. He shifted her weight under one arm—as if she were a child, she thought furiously—opened the far door of the van, and dumped her on the seat. The door slammed. She saw his profile cross in front of the lights again and then he had opened the other door and climbed in beside her. As he shut his own door rather more quietly than he had shut hers, and turned on the overhead light, Roslin found her voice. 'What the *devil* do you think you're doing?' she croaked.

His grin had elements of the demonic. 'Trying not to catch pneumonia.'

'A better way would have been to have minded your own business and driven to your precious camp-ground. By yourself!'

'Before you get to the village I mentioned, there's a farmer whose dogs are known to be vicious and which aren't always kept tied up the way they should be,' he rapped. 'There's also a family in the village of whose sons two have been charged with sexual assault.'

Once again Roslin knew he was telling the truth. 'Oh,' she said, then was disgusted with herself for such a weak response.

'Women's lib is all very well, but if you're five feet five and weigh less than a hundred pounds you should exercise a little common sense——'

'Kindly don't lecture me!'

'—or take a course in karate.'

Living with Colby, she had not needed a course in karate. Nor would she have had the time to take one, she added to herself. One of her uncle's tactics had been to keep her so busy she had not had the time to think. She said stiffly, 'I weigh one hundred and thirteen pounds and I'm five feet five and three-quarters.'

'A veritable Amazon,' the man said, with a genuine amusement that warmed and deepened his voice. 'Why don't you take off that poncho and put your pack on the floor? You'd be a lot more comfortable.'

It was sensible advice, and she would be silly not to take it just because it came from him. Roslin hauled the wet folds of the poncho over her head and bent to deposit her backpack on the floor of the van. Then she sat up, turning to face her rescuer.

'Good lord,' he said quietly.

Roslin was used to this reaction, for not even Colby had been able to isolate her totally from the male half of the population. 'Don't make remarks about launching a thousand ships, don't say my profile reminds you of Nefertiti, and don't ask me if I'm a model,' she ordered.

He was still staring at her, and she knew well enough from her own mirror what he was seeing. Her hair, bundled into a pigtail, was that rare, true black that contained within it the sheen of midnight-blue, while her eyes, too dark to be called blue, too blue to be called black, were like deep, mysterious pools. The austerity of hollowed cheekbones and straight black brows were belied by the curve of her lips, soft and full of promise. Roslin herself had often tried to be cold-blooded about her looks, reducing them to a catalogue of features that taken individually were pleasant but not startling; what she missed in these inventories was the allure of the tilted eyes, and the unconscious invitation of the vulnerable mouth and slender neck with its burden of gleaming hair.

Colby had used her looks; the television production two months ago had brought that to a head, although she had known it subconsciously for a long time. Since her precipitate flight from Boston she had decided to play down her appearance as much as possible, so that she would be taken for herself rather than for some goddess who promised the unattainable. Hence the pigtail, the total lack of make-up, and the unbecoming poncho.

None of which had worked. Obviously.

Turning her face away from the man at the wheel and gazing at the windscreen down which the rain was now streaming, she said with a catch in her voice, 'I was so enjoying being alone...'

He said coldly, 'So, as it happens, was I.'

Roslin transferred her gaze back to his face. It was set grimly; he did not look like a man about to succumb to her charms. In fact, he looked as though he would like to thrust her back on to the road and drive off as fast as he could. 'You're already regretting your good deed, aren't you?' she asked, and not for the first time in her life cursed her looks.

'You could say so.'

'Once we get to the camp-ground I'll leave you to yourself.'

'You'll put up the tent and use the sleeping-bag you've got tucked away in your pack,' he answered sarcastically.

Her pack contained a minimal wardrobe, a book and a few toilet articles. Roslin snapped, 'They must have cabins to rent.'

'They don't. I go there because it's undeveloped.'

And because you want to be alone, she added silently, suddenly aware that she was cold, hungry and tired. 'Look, you're the one who insisted I get in the van— it's a bit late to change your mind now,' she said, sounding much less forceful than she had intended.

'Take responsibility for your actions,' he recited grimly. 'I learned that one a long time ago.' Putting the van in first gear, he automatically checked the rear-view mirror. 'My name's Tyson McCully. Yours is...?'

'Roslin Hebb.'

'Roslin suits you,' he said, his attention on the holes in the road. 'Am I to be told why you're wandering along a dead-end road in the middle of a rainstorm?'

She put her head to one side. 'I was planning on launching the fishing fleet from Penisquit?'

'All four Cape Islanders? You underrate yourself, Miss Hebb.'

'Even Mozart didn't start off with a symphony,' said Roslin, then could have bitten off her tongue. Music was no longer part of her life; she must not even think about it.

'Far too many people think small in this life.'

'I scarcely think you're one of them.'

'I wouldn't have thought you were, either.'

He had touched a sore spot. 'One has to tailor one's ambitions to the cold winds of reality,' she said bitterly.

'You can be so busy reaching for the stars, you fall flat on your face.'

'Such cynicism in one so young,' he remarked, but his eyes were very shrewd.

Cursing herself for getting involved in this conversation, Roslin said, 'Why don't you describe the campground for me, Mr McCully?'

'The name's Tyson. If we're going to spend the night together, let's at least be on a first-name basis.'

She didn't like the sound of that remark. But campgrounds had cooking shelters, and surely he would lend her a sleeping-bag? 'You've been here before, haven't you?'

'Several times.'

She clutched her seat as the van lurched through a series of pot-holes. 'This isn't the kind of night most people would choose to go camping,' she said provocatively.

It was she who had touched the nerve this time. 'The van's my escape route,' he said tightly. 'When everything starts crowding in on me, I take off and forget about the rest of the world.'

'Freedom,' she said, more to herself than to him.

'The illusion of freedom,' he replied mockingly. 'Haven't you learned the difference yet, Roslin Hebb?'

'I don't plan to learn the difference—I want the real thing,' she said, with a desperate intensity that was very revealing.

He glanced over at her. She met his eyes, her own blazing with purpose. He said slowly, 'So you know what it's like to feel the world closing in on you...' Suddenly he smiled. 'You'll like the camp-ground, Roslin. Not everyone would—but you will.'

He had not smiled properly before. She gulped, for the van seemed too small to contain such energy, such purely masculine charisma: devil transformed to Don Juan. He looked much younger when he smiled, she thought, trying to be prosaic. He also looked devastatingly attractive.

'So at ten o'clock at night you got this sudden urge for freedom?' she said with genuine curiosity.

'None of your business, my dear.' As she flushed, he added, 'I'm quite sure if I asked you why you were going to Buckton, which is one of those self-consciously artsy little towns complete with Gift Shoppes and Tea Shoppes and Ye Olde Village Inns, not your kind of place at all, you would give me the same reply.'

She would have to, because she was not going to Buckton. Many years ago her mother had warned her against lying. 'One lie leads to another, Roslin,' she had said. 'And your nature is not naturally devious—music tends to force one to the truth, doesn't it? So leave the lies to others; you'll only trip yourself up.'

Briefly Roslin closed her eyes, still able to see the wry smile on her mother's beautiful face...

'What's wrong?' Tyson said sharply.

'Nothing!'

Skilfully he eased the vehicle over a miniature ditch that the rain had carved in the road. 'I suggest we get something straight right now. We can discuss freedom in the abstract, but we won't ask personal details about each other—agreed?'

Since the death of her parents she had had no one with whom to share the worries, the tensions and the victories of her day-to-day life. So why should she feel disappointed that a total stranger had also repudiated the role of confidant? 'That seems sensible,' she said coolly.

'Good. Ah, there's the bridge, five minutes to go.'

In slightly less than five minutes Roslin saw a light pierce the darkness, and then saw a worn wooden sign that was swinging madly in the wind as if it too longed to be free. Tyson braked, and said in a peculiar voice, 'I always come here alone—and Buck's the type to put the worst possible interpretation on my arriving at night in the company of a beautiful young woman.'

For some reason Roslin had pictured the owners as an elderly couple in mail-order clothes who would be happy to rent her a room for the night. 'Buck?' she repeated.

'A very appropriate name. He's a bachelor who doesn't believe in washing dishes or the kitchen floor, that's women's work. Trouble is, he can usually find himself a woman gullible enough to do it for him. In return for certain favours.'

She would have to stay in the cooking shelter. 'I'll hide on the floor of the van if you want to preserve your reputation,' she said sweetly.

He scowled at her. 'Aren't you worried about yours?'

Fluttering her lashes, she said, 'I don't know a soul in Penisquit. And we don't have to tell him I'll be sleeping in the cooking shelter.'

'Roslin, this camp-ground does not have cooking shelters. Or any other kind of shelters. The washrooms are outhouses, the water comes from a hand-pump, and there's no electricity. I told you it was primitive.' His smile was derisive. 'So you've got your choice. Buck or me.'

She tilted her chin. 'I see what you mean by the illusion of freedom.'

He laughed. 'You'll be far safer with me.'

'Plus you don't have a kitchen floor.'

His mouth twisted. 'Not here, anyway.'

'Are you married?' Roslin said suspiciously.

'I'd call that a personal question, wouldn't you, Miss Hebb?'

'You don't look married.'

'I can see this is going to be a long night,' Tyson remarked, putting the van in gear and driving towards the sign. 'To hell with Buck, let him think what he wants.'

'I do admire courage in a man,' Roslin said soulfully.

'A very long night.' Tyson turned right by the sign
and pulled up in front of a house that could be described
charitably as quaint or uncharitably as decrepit; the door
opened so quickly that Roslin was sure Buck had been
watching their approach. He crossed in front of the van
as Tyson lowered the window.

Swathed in oilskins, unshaven and smelling strongly
of rum, Buck was not an appealing figure. Nor was she
impressed by his leer as he caught sight of her. 'Hey, got
yourself a filly!' he drawled, giving Tyson a comradely
punch on the arm. 'A right cute little one at that. 'Bout
time, I'd say, don't do a man no good to spend too much
time on his own. What's your name, sweetie?'

'Joan Sutherland,' she snapped.

'How de do, Joanie. Take any spot you like, Tyson,
the place is pretty near empty and you'll want to be off
by yourselves, won't you?' He winked at Roslin. 'Don't
rock the van, honey.'

She opened her mouth to reply, her cheeks scarlet.
Quickly Tyson intervened. 'Thanks, Buck. See you
tomorrow,' he said, and drove down the gravel track.

'You call that a choice?' Roslin bleated.

'Makes me look good, huh?'

'I'll say.' She peered through the window as the tyres
sent up a sheet of spray; all she could see was rain and
spruce trees. 'Is it a personal question if I ask where
we're going?'

'Down near the sea. I like waking up to the sound of
the surf.'

Although they were passing open patches of grass,
there were no other campers parked in the shelter of the
trees. With a pang of fear, Roslin wondered if she would
not have been wiser to have braved the vicious dogs and
the dubious young men in the village rather than find
herself in this deserted camp-ground with Buck as her
sole source of help. What, after all, did she know about
Tyson McCully?

She would be the first to admit she was not streetwise; she had had very little chance with Colby overlooking her every move. Was she about to become a statistic, yet another young woman found dead after being foolish enough to take a ride from an unknown man? Her muscles tensed, and her right hand felt for the Italian dagger at her waist. Tyson was strong, she knew that much about him, for he had picked her up as though she weighed less than nothing. In her heart of hearts she did not think the dagger would be much use.

The van jerked to a halt. Her pulse gave an exaggerated leap. Tyson switched off the headlights, blanking out the wind-torn trees and the needles of rain, and turned on a small overhead light. 'Roslin, look at me,' he said.

The pale light fell on her wide-held eyes and the defensive hunch of her shoulders. He said forcibly, 'You don't have to look so frightened. I promise I won't hurt you in any way—I won't lay a hand on you. Please believe me.'

Almost, she did. If only he weren't quite so large, so broad of chest, so overpoweringly male, she thought in dismay. If only she herself were not so totally inexperienced. Out of her depth in waters as murky as the puddles outside.

'Do you believe me?' Tyson persisted.

Her eyes wavered. 'I suppose so.'

'I happen to like my women willing,' he said, not bothering to mask his anger. 'Odd of me, I agree, but we all have our hang-ups. Frightened rabbits don't turn me on.'

Roslin bit her lip, her lashes sweeping her cheek as she gazed down at the twisted fingers in her lap. 'How tall are you, Tyson?' she asked in a low voice.

'Six feet one.'

'And if you'll excuse another personal question, how much do you weigh?'

'One hundred and eighty...I know what you're getting at, Roslin—equality is fine until you take the physical into account, we've all heard it a hundred times. I guess I just don't like being treated like a potential rapist.'

She did not look up. 'I'm sorry,' she muttered.

He hesitated. Then, reaching across, he rested one hand on hers. 'Apology accepted.'

His hand was beautifully shaped, though marred with scars and rough with calluses. It was also clean, warm and strangely comforting. But, as her fingers relaxed a little, he snatched his hand away. She blurted, 'You don't touch people very often, do you?'

'You sure ask a lot of questions,' he said nastily. 'Put on your poncho and I'll show you the amenities, such as they are. Then I'll make some hot chocolate and cinnamon toast before we settle down for the night.'

No rapist that she had ever heard of had prefaced his crime with cinnamon toast. And she had not eaten since noon. Roslin pulled the clammy raingear over her head, opened her door and slid down to the ground.

CHAPTER TWO

AS THE wind buffeted her, Roslin was assailed by a new noise, a dull, rhythmic roar, and tasted the sting of salt on her lips. The sea, she thought in wonder. It was years since she had walked the length of a beach in summer . . .

Tyson seized her sleeve. 'This way,' he shouted.

She forgot that she was supposed to be afraid of him. 'Can we go and see the waves?' she shouted back.

Colby would have recoiled in horror. 'Sure!' said Tyson, grinning at her as he did up the snaps on his yellow rain slicker. 'Do you like storms?'

She nodded, tugging at his arm impatiently. 'Let's go.'

Side by side, Tyson lighting the way with a flashlight, they plunged through the wet grass, which in places was knee-deep, and as they went the voice of the sea grew louder. They left the last spruce tree behind, climbing a slight slope, Roslin's poncho trailing behind her like the tail of a comet. When they reached an untidy heap of rocks, Tyson grabbed her arm again. 'Careful,' he yelled. 'Sounds like high tide.'

She braced herself on the bank, staring out into the darkness. Serried waves reared up from the blackness of the sea. The tumbled surf as it broke on the rocks glowed with an eerie white light, hissing and seething in its age-old attack on the land, retreating in rampant disorder and a rattle of stones that was like a thousand castanets.

This was why she had left Colby, Roslin thought, swept by excitement. This was why she had run away. She pulled free of Tyson's hold, impulsively ripping the ribbon from her hair and shaking it free of its thick braid, so that it whipped around her head. Closing her eyes, mingled spray and rain beating against her face, she gave herself up to the majestic symphony that was the music of the ocean.

When, eventually, she looked over at her companion, her features were brilliant with exhilaration, her waist-long hair wrapped about her neck like seaweed. '*This* is freedom,' she cried. 'No illusions here, Tyson—this is real!'

He was staring at her as if he had never seen a woman before. Grasping her by the shoulders, so his fingers were streaked with her hair, he said fiercely, 'Who are you? Where have you come from?'

Drunk by the onslaught of sound, of a myriad sounds like a percussionist gone mad, Roslin laughed up at him. 'I'm a sea-witch...be careful, I might vanish into the storm, and all you'll ever hear of me will be the cry of the wind when you come to the shore.'

He tightened his hold. 'You won't vanish—I won't let you,' he said roughly. Bending his head, he kissed her hard on the mouth, as though the human warmth of his lips would break the spell she had cast.

He could have been a god cast up by the waves. Roslin was pliant in his embrace, the kiss an elemental joining that had all the violence and passion of the storm that raged both within her and around her. But then his arms went hard about her body, and he groaned deep in his throat, and for Roslin the brief madness was over. Suddenly overwhelmed with panic, she fought against him, writhing in his arms; to her infinite relief he slackened his hold.

She backed away from him. The flashlight had fallen to the ground; his features, blurred by the rain, were taut with a mixture of emotions she could not have begun to name. 'You mustn't do that again!' she gasped. 'You said you wouldn't touch me.'

Tyson gave his head a little shake, looking around him with the air of a man not sure where he was. Then he brought his eyes back to her face; they were as black as the sky. 'Don't worry, I won't,' he swore. 'I don't know what happened to me . . . Let's get out of here.'

After stooping to pick up the flashlight, he turned his back on the tormented ocean and strode down the slope, his body bent against the wind. He did not look back to see if she was following. Roslin was frightened of him, but she had no desire to spend the night on the beach. She scurried after him, trying to blot from her mind the scorching memory of his lips against hers in a kiss that had been unlike any other she had ever received.

The amenities, as Tyson had euphemistically labelled them, were undoubtedly primitive. Roslin was glad to return to the van, to the pocket of shelter and warmth it represented. She had been a fool to get her hair so wet, a fool to babble on about sea-witches and freedom . . . for one traitorous moment she longed to be back in her bed in the old house in Boston.

Tyson slid open a door in the side of the van and gestured for her to precede him; she climbed in, heard the door bang shut, and slowly straightened. She was in the main part of the vehicle, behind the seats. As Tyson struck a match and lit a propane lamp, she looked around her.

At any other time the van would have enchanted her. It had cupboards, bookshelves, and a built-in refrigerator, plaid curtains at the windows and a carpet on the floor; it was spotlessly clean. She said helplessly, 'I'll get everything wet.'

With practised movements Tyson pushed up a canvas and metal roof, so that even he could stand upright. 'Give me your poncho,' he said.

Roslin dragged it off and passed it to him. He hung it over one of the roof bars, hanging his own jacket beside it. 'There's a mat for shoes. Do you have any dry clothes?'

Her pack contained a skirt and blouse for her meeting with the lawyer, a tank top and a pair of shorts, and a nightgown that she had chosen for its light weight rather

than its modesty. 'Yes,' she mumbled, wishing she had
brought her fleecy tracksuit.

'You'd better get out of those wet things while I make
the hot chocolate.'

She reached round the passenger seat for her pack,
banging her elbow as she did so. The tank top was brief
and the nightgown indecent; it would have to be the skirt
and blouse. She aligned her soggy sneakers neatly on the
mat and looped her mud-stained socks over the rail. Then
she stopped. Tyson's back was perhaps eight inches from
her. The floor space measured no more than six feet by
six. And she had never in her life undressed in the
presence of a man.

She said in a strangled voice, 'Please don't turn
around.'

He was lifting what she had presumed was a counter-
top to reveal a small propane stove and a tiny sink.
Taking his time, he anchored the metal props. 'I won't,'
he said.

She yanked her jeans down her legs, the dagger still
fastened to one of the belt loops. Leaving the jeans in
a heap on the carpet, she hastily unbuttoned her damp
shirt and flung it to the floor too. Her fingers awkward
with haste, she then slipped into the blouse and skirt,
which she had chosen because they did not crease, and
struggled with the buttons. The clothes seemed to armour
her against her fears. She draped the jeans and shirt over
the roof rack and said, 'I'll need a towel, my hair's wet.'

Tyson had knelt to open the door of the refrigerator,
his spine a long curve, his jeans tight across his thighs.
'In the cupboard over the couch,' he said without turning
around.

The cupboard contained towels and shaving gear.
Roslin selected a fluffy blue towel. 'I'm decent now,' she
said in a small voice.

Tyson glanced over his shoulder. She was combing
her hair to one side of her head with her fingers, the
bright floral print of her blouse rippling as she moved,

her legs and high-arched feet bare. Her skin had a pearl-like pallor. Picking up the towel, she began scrubbing at her hair. After a barely perceptible pause, Tyson said, 'You haven't spent much time in the sun.'

'I...I've been studying,' Roslin prevaricated, her voice muffled. 'No chance to laze around in the sun. But that's going to change.' With a gasp of relief she emerged from the thickness of the towel, bent to get her brush and started pulling it through her hair, a routine she had followed since she was a child.

The long, silky strands seemed to seize the lamplight so that they glimmered and shone with a life of their own. Without ceremony Roslin gathered them into a loose braid, fastening the end with a band she took from the pocket of her skirt. Then, alerted by the quality of the silence, she looked up. Tyson said hoarsely, 'You should always wear your hair loose.'

She found that her back was pressed against the side of the van. 'It's too much trouble,' she said, and knew the words they were speaking had nothing to do with the naked hunger in the man's eyes. 'My mother never wanted me to cut it,' she prattled on, 'so I never have. But it can be an awful nuisance. Especially when you're swimming.'

He had lost that blinded look, although the pulse was still pounding at the base of his throat and the hand gripping the saucepan was white-knuckled. He took a deep breath and said levelly, 'I'll put the milk on—keep an eye on it, will you, while I get out of this wet shirt?'

Roslin edged around him to take position by the stove, her attention glued to the saucepan of milk. She heard the whisper of cotton as he took off his shirt, and the rattle of metal as he hung it over the bar. There was a small silence. Then he said tersely, 'What's that on your jeans?'

The dagger. She should have hidden it. 'Mud?' she said facetiously.

'It's a knife of some kind.'

'It's a seventeenth-century Italian dagger that belonged to my father,' she explained with rather overdone patience. 'I've been hitch-hiking from Boston—I figured I might need it.'

'Are you in trouble with the law?'

'No! Of course not.' The milk forgotten, Roslin whirled to face him, indignation written all over her.

He was naked to the waist, the jeans slung low on his hips. Muscle flowed over bone, taut muscles flat to his body, economical and beautiful; she was reminded instantly of Michelangelo's statue of David, which she had seen three months ago in Florence. Had she been able to rest her palm against David's curving shoulder, the stone would have drawn all the heat from her hand, whereas if she were to rest her hand on Tyson's body, she would meet the warmth of living flesh, the ripple of movement, the roughness of hair. For Tyson was very much alive...

He said in a voice that was unaccountably angry, 'Stop acting as if you've never seen a half-naked man before.'

How could she put into words her confused sensations? For Roslin did indeed feel as if something in her had been waiting for this moment, in order that she begin to understand what a man was, and how he could affect her. Aloysha had been a marvellous companion, and she had loved the sense of power when she had light-heartedly flirted with him. But she had not had this violent urge to touch Aloysha, this primitive desire to feel, to explore, to discover. That, too, would be an expression of freedom...

She gasped, 'I'm not used to being this close to one,' and heard behind her the sizzle of boiling milk. With an incoherent exclamation she lifted the saucepan off the stove. 'Where's the chocolate?'

From a cupboard over her head Tyson took a couple of mugs and spoons and a foil envelope; Roslin was thus presented with a close-up view of his ribs and with the clean, wholly masculine scent of his skin. She closed her eyes and said, 'I do wish you'd put a shirt on.'

Mugs and spoons clattered on the counter-top, making her jump. Tyson snarled, 'You're as damned aware of me as I am of you.'

Her eyes snapped open. 'You don't have to swear!'

He tossed the envelope of chocolate powder on the counter and grabbed her by the arm. 'Believe it or not, this has never happened to me before. I've been attracted to women, don't get me wrong—but I've never in my life met someone and five minutes later felt like tearing the clothes from her body and making love to her on the floor. I don't know the first thing about you, for heaven's sake!'

His eyes were not black, she noticed numbly. They were grey, stormy as the sea on a winter's day, turbulent with emotion. 'We are not going to make love on the floor,' she retorted.

He pushed her away so strongly that she staggered. 'I don't need you in my life, do you hear me? I've got the next few months all mapped out and I don't want my plans disrupted. Couldn't you have taken any other road in Maine but the one to the camp-ground?'

Roslin should have replied with restraint and calmness and logic. Instead she lost her temper. 'So it's all my fault! Well, I don't need you any more than you need me, Tyson McCully. Tomorrow morning you can drop me off at the main road and forget you ever met me, and next time maybe you won't be quite so quick to throw someone in your van just because it's raining. And, for your information, I'm planning to cut my hair as soon as I get to a decent stylist.'

'*No!*'

The word had been torn from him entirely without his volition, Roslin was sure. She watched him rake his fingers through his hair and heard him mutter, 'This is ludicrous. What you do with your hair has nothing to do with me.'

'That's right,' she said steadily, and, because he looked so beleaguered and unhappy, added with a gleam of humour, 'Neither you nor my mother has to cope with all the tangles after I've been swimming. Please can we have the hot chocolate, Tyson? Before it's cold chocolate?'

'Yeah...'

He reheated the milk, then added the powdered chocolate and stirred the milk into the mugs; he was glad to have something to do, she knew, and sat down on the narrow couch with her feet tucked under her. If someone had told her two days ago that she would find herself in this situation, she would have told them they were crazy. Freedom, she was discovering, could lead one in strange paths.

Tyson passed her a mug, then rummaged in the overhead cupboard for a T-shirt, which he pulled on before sitting down beside her. They sipped the drink in silence. The rain pattered on the roof. The wind howled. And all the while Roslin tried to think of something to say that would both ignore what had just happened and betray no curiosity about the man sitting so close to her. Finally, unable to bear the silence any longer, she said, 'You forgot the cinnamon toast.'

'Are you hungry?'

'Starving. I had a greasy hamburger at a truck stop approximately eleven hours ago.'

'I'll make you something to eat. It'll beat sitting here and bursting with questions I know I shouldn't ask. Shouldn't even want to ask.' But instead of getting up he encircled her wrist with one hand, tracing the blue veins under her skin with the other. Roslin held her breath, aware of his touch with every nerve in her body. She was no longer afraid of him, she realised. But she was afraid of herself.

He said quietly, 'Part of me wants to find out everything about you...how old you are, where you're going, whether you've ever been in love, what kind of ice-cream you like, on and on the questions go. The other part says, none of your business, Tyson, she's nothing to do with you, just a chance meeting that you can't allow to disrupt your life, and so what if she prefers strawberry ice-cream to maple walnut.' Without changing his voice he went on, 'I feel as though I'm holding a bird in my hand—your pulse is racing like the heart of a bird and your skin is as soft as the feathers on a bird's breast.'

She whispered, 'That's the most beautiful thing anyone has ever said to me.'

His thumb caressed the tendons in her wrist. 'You understand how I'm feeling, don't you, Roslin? Because you feel the same way.'

She could be nothing but honest. 'Tyson, for a number of reasons I've had very little experience of men—you must take that on trust. Yes, I feel something. In some ways I feel as though I've known you all my life, even though I know virtually nothing about you. But maybe I'd feel that way with anyone right now, because I'm tasting freedom for the first time in years and it's a heady wine, freedom...' Then she did what she had been longing to do ever since he had stripped off his shirt; she cupped his shoulder in her palm, and felt the warmth of his flesh seep through the fabric of his T-shirt.

For a moment they remained frozen, grey eyes locked with midnight-blue. Then Tyson dropped her wrist and stood up so swiftly that her hand flopped back on the couch. 'I'll make some toast,' he said.

What he was really saying was that he would ask no questions. That she was not to be allowed to disrupt his life. Whatever that implied. Roslin sat very still, swirling the chocolate in her mug. He must be married, she thought blankly. If he had a wife he could not very well pursue a chance-met stranger, no matter how strongly she attracted him. Wondering what his wife was like, deciding that she, Roslin, would thoroughly dislike her, she accepted two pieces of toast, chewed them mechanically, and helped Tyson clear away the dishes, all in a stony silence.

When everything was put away, he pulled on a strap beneath the couch, which flattened it out to make it part of a mattress that stretched back between the rear wheels. He took sheets from a side cupboard Roslin had not noticed before and methodically tucked them in, spreading a quilt on top of them; the resulting bed was somewhere between a single and a double.

Roslin had been watching. She said awkwardly, 'Where's the other bed?'

He threw a couple of pillows against the rear window. 'There's only one.'

'But—I can't sleep with you!'

He stood up. 'You'll have to—there's nowhere else.'

'I thought the table folded out and made a bed.'

'No, Roslin, it doesn't.'

His Roman general look was back. She could not sleep on the floor, for the extension of the couch had further diminished its size. 'I'll sit up all night,' she said defiantly.

'Don't be silly. And don't behave like a stereotypical female, Roslin—you aren't one. We're going to get in bed and go to sleep, and in the morning we'll go our separate ways ... If it'll make you feel better I'll put out the lamp before you get undressed.'

She said faintly, 'I chose the nightdress I've got with me because it doesn't take up any room in my pack and it weighs practically nothing. I am not putting it on, regardless of whether the light is on or off. You'll have to lend me a pair of pyjamas.'

Tyson raised one brow. 'I haven't got any.'

'A shirt, then.'

'My only other shirt is wet.'

She glowered at him. 'What are *you* wearing to bed?'

'Wouldn't you say that falls in the category of a personal question?'

'Tyson McCully,' she seethed, 'you don't have to make it quite so clear that you're enjoying this. And I don't care what category the question falls in. Just answer it!'

There was a gleam of pure devilment in his eye. 'I was planning to wear my shorts and T-shirt. But you can borrow the T-shirt if you like.'

It would cover her far more adequately than the nightgown. 'I accept,' she said.

'Shall I put out the light?'

'Please do,' Roslin answered loftily, fighting against a reprehensible urge to burst out laughing. But it could well be hysterical laughter, she knew. In future she would be more careful how she used the word 'freedom'.

The lamp stood on the folding table by the bed. Tyson eased around her in the cramped floor space and turned down the wick. The light faded to a tiny white glow, then disappeared altogether. 'You get undressed first and I'll pass you the T-shirt,' he said helpfully.

'Turn your back.'

As he complied, she wriggled out of her skirt and blouse, leaving on the lacy underwear she had also chosen for its flimsiness. 'OK,' she said.

The darkness was not absolute; Roslin could see the outline of his torso as Tyson peeled off his T-shirt. He thrust it at her behind his back. It was warm from his body, a warmth that stroked her flesh with fire as she pulled the garment over her head. It reached only to the tops of her thighs, although it would have encompassed two of her, width-wise.

Ducking between the wet clothes, she arranged her skirt and blouse on the passenger seat before climbing on the bed. 'This *is* a very personal question,' she said, aware again of that bubble of hysteria. 'Which side of the bed do you sleep on?'

'The middle,' he replied blandly.

The scrape of his zipper sounded very loud. Roslin scrambled under the covers, pulling them up to her chin. 'Tyson, stop playing games! The right side or the left?'

'Right.'

The mattress at the end of the bed sagged as he put his weight on it, and even in the darkness Roslin could discern the bulk of his body. In a flash of sheer terror she cowered against the wall, dragging the quilt with her.

He grew still, crouched partway up the bed. 'What's the matter?'

She felt humiliatingly close to tears and her voice seemed to have disappeared. Colby or no Colby, she would have given all of Great-Aunt Mellicent's inheritance to find herself back in the house where she had grown up with her parents.

Tyson said flatly, 'Roslin, if it will make you feel better, I'll pass you that nasty little Italian dagger and you can clutch it to your bosom all night. But I assure you you won't need it—I'm tired and I'm going to sleep.'

He had already mentioned frightened rabbits and stereotypical females; he had only to bring up terrified virgins and she would burst into tears. 'I know I'm being silly,' she quavered.

In the darkness his voice sounded oddly gentle. 'Haven't you ever slept with a man before?'

'Inexperienced was the word I used,' she wailed. 'Of course I haven't!'

'In this day and age there's no "of course" about it. Although the men in Boston must be blind. Roslin, dear, you're safer in this van than you'd be anywhere else in the world, I swear to that. Now lie down and go to sleep.'

His endearment tugged at her heartstrings, so that again she could very easily have burst into tears. She burrowed under the quilt, facing the wall, and felt Tyson get in beside her. He too turned his face to the wall. 'Goodnight, Roslin,' he said. 'Sleep well.'

'You, too,' she murmured.

Five minutes ago she had been convinced she would not sleep a wink. But the patter of rain on the roof was a peaceful sound, and through the sigh of the wind she could hear the distant roar of the breakers on the shore.

The bed was warm. Tyson was breathing steadily beside her, and with faint incredulity she realised that that was a peaceful sound as well. She shut her eyes, deciding she would listen until she was sure he was no longer awake, and with the suddenness of a child she fell asleep.

A bird was singing right over her head. A bird with feathers as soft as her skin...

But the skin under her cheek was rough with hairs. A weight was thrown over one leg; an arm appeared to be resting on her ribs. Roslin's eyes flew open.

The narrow little bed in the van was suffused with the soft light of early dawn. The rain had stopped and the wind had died, so the rhythmic fall of the waves sounded very close. Sunshine peeped coyly through a chink in the curtains.

All these impressions flashed through Roslin's mind in the fraction of a second. Then she forgot them. Her cheek was lying in the crook of Tyson's elbow, and his breath stirred her hair. In the night each had turned to the other, and it was his thigh that held her pinioned and his arm that loosely embraced her. He was deeply asleep.

She, in contrast, was shocked to wakefulness. She lay very still and, perhaps because she was not sure she could cope with this unexpected physical intimacy, she focused on Tyson's face. Sleep altered it in a way that she struggled to define. He looked younger, more approachable, and not at all like a Roman general. So what was missing?

A certain tension, she decided thoughtfully. A guardedness that she had not really recognised until it was no longer there. Awake, he had the air of a man who had had to fight for what he wanted and fight hard, depending only on himself, never allowing himself to relax or show his vulnerability. Loneliness, she added in a flash of intuition, warming to her subject. That was it. He was a loner.

She found herself wondering what had shaped him, what betrayals and deprivations had led to an aggression she knew he could not always control. Not everyone would tuck a young woman under his arm, no matter how hard it was raining or how admirable his motives.

His chest rose and fell with his breathing, as physical and dependable a rhythm as that of the surf on the beach. The bird carolled overhead with the dedicated enthusiasm of an opera singer. Then Tyson stirred a little in his sleep, his arm drawing her nearer so that her body touched the length of his, their legs more closely entwined; she could have reached up and kissed the relaxed curve of his mouth, or smoothed the small crescent-shaped scar over one eye, a scar she had not noticed before.

Roslin did neither of these things. She was sure that at some level Tyson would resent her scrutiny of his sleeping, unguarded features, that it would seem an invasion of his privacy were he to wake and find her staring at him. So she nestled her head more comfortably into his shoulder and composed herself for sleep.

But sleep did not come easily this time. The T-shirt she was wearing had ridden up during the night so that her bare flesh was pressed against his, and the heaviness of his thigh aroused the same sensations she had felt last night, the powerful, all-consuming urge to stroke and explore. Her body felt fluid, melting into his; she thought of the lovers in Rodin's 'The Kiss', and of the innocent wonder with which she had studied that sculpture. She understood better now the forces that had drawn those lovers together so completely and so hungrily, for the same forces seemed to have her in their grip: she had lost her innocence. Squeezing her eyes shut, she began going through the score of Beethoven's last sonata note by note.

She fell asleep.

She dreamed of a sculpture-garden in which the carved figures stepped down from their pedestals and embraced each other, stone melting to flesh. A helmeted general was stroking her shoulder, grey eyes mesmerising her to submission...

Roslin pushed against him and woke up.

CHAPTER THREE

TYSON was facing Roslin, leaning on one elbow as he tugged her hair loose of its braid, his face intent on his task. Their bodies were no longer touching. Remembering how she had fallen asleep wrapped in his arms, Roslin flushed scarlet and jerked her head away.

He said almost matter-of-factly, 'I'll never see you again after today, Roslin—I wanted to see your hair loose on the pillow just this once.' But then the façade vanished as he added with barely suppressed violence, 'If you were naked, I would wrap it around you like a cloak.'

Her body sprang to life. Her eyes, more blue than black, blazed into his as the acknowledgement of passion flared between them, age-old, intensely personal, immediate.

I am yours, she told him silently. Take me, I beg of you.

The turbulent grey eyes responded with their own message of desire. I would bring you joy such as you have never known, they seemed to be saying, and in the giving find my own fulfilment.

So was this freedom, Roslin thought helplessly, to do whatever she wanted when she wanted regardless of the consequences? Her head drooped, her hair falling to hide her face. 'I can't, Tyson,' she said.

'We can't,' he corrected her evenly. 'But at least we were honest enough to admit we wanted each other.'

She looked up, and inexplicably her eyes were full of tears. 'It's the funniest thing,' she said. 'In this short time—what is it, less than twelve hours?—you've changed my life. I'll never forget you.'

The grimness was back in his mouth and the distance in his eyes. 'I rather doubt I'll forget you, either.'

The tears would overflow if she stayed with him in the intimacy of the narrow bed any longer. She kicked her legs free of the covers and said breathlessly, 'I'm going to walk to the shore; I won't be long.' She could have added that she needed to be alone, but with Tyson she did not think she had to.

Her jeans were still wet, encrusted with mud. So it would have to be the shorts in her pack. She hauled them on, seeing from the corner of her eye that Tyson had rather ostentatiously turned on his stomach, his head buried in his arms. Keeping on his T-shirt, because somehow she could not bear to take it off, she unlatched the side door of the van and stepped down bare-footed on to the wet grass.

Droplets of rain still hung like crystals on the spruce boughs, refracting the morning sun into all the colours of the rainbow; in a great flutter of wings two robins launched themselves from the tree into the pale blue sky. The air was pure and sweet, and the line between sea and sky gleamed like the blade of the Italian dagger. Roslin began to walk, watching for stones underfoot, feasting her eyes on the white starbursts of daisies in the field and the tangled, pink-spattered rosebushes that edged the perimeter of the camp-ground. It was going to be a beautiful day. A perfect day to arrive in Carmel and lay claim to her inheritance.

Perfect except for Tyson, she thought unhappily.

Tyson had no intentions of following up on this chance meeting, he had made that very clear. She was a complicating factor in a life about which she knew almost nothing. Not his age, nor his address, nor his marital status. Not his job nor his background.

She knew he was in flight from something. And she knew he desired her.

This did not seem very much on which to base a future relationship. And she was quite sure, after the few hours they had spent together, that he would treat any questions with evasions or blunt denial.

She had reached the shore. In daylight she could see the sweep of a pebbled beach heaped with seaweed from the storm and pounded by waves that still held the energy of last night's wind in their tumbled foam. Further out, the ocean was a brilliant blue-green.

Roslin sat down on a rock, cupping her chin in her hands, and tried very hard to empty her mind of all her concerns: Tyson, Colby, the grand piano in the house in Boston, Great-Aunt Mellicent who had left her a property by the sea and who, indirectly, had led to a long-due rebellion. She was going to see that property today. If she liked it, she was going to live there. And to hell with Colby and his plans for her future career as a concert pianist, she thought mutinously. At this precise moment she didn't care if she ever saw a piano again, let alone played one.

Discovering that she did not want to think about Colby any more than she wanted to think about Tyson, she stooped and picked up a shell from among the sea-rounded pebbles, holding it to her ear; from its spiral coils came the ancient whisper of the ocean. The sun fell hot on her shoulders. A seagull, blindingly white, drifted over the flotsam on the beach. Time passed.

As had so often happened in the past, the silence in Roslin's mind became filled with music. This time it was a melody new to her, a simple melody in a minor key with a haunting refrain. How many times in the last few months had she been distracted by such melodies, and how many times had Colby driven her back to the keyboard to practise, practise, practise! Rummaging in her shorts' pockets, Roslin found a scrap of paper and the stub of a pencil, things she rarely travelled without. Her fingers flew across the page, the melody embellishing itself, suggesting variations and changes of key... She would have to try it out on the piano...

The pencil dug into the paper. She did not have a piano. She had turned her back on the Steinway in the studio in Boston and on all that it represented. In a sudden gesture of revulsion she tore the paper in shreds and scattered the pieces on the stones. Let the sea take them—they were nothing to do with her.

Restlessly she got up from the rock and wandered back to the field, where she plucked a small bouquet of wild flowers and long-stemmed grasses. Then she heard Tyson calling her name, and when she looked around saw him waving to her from the grove of evergreens where he had parked the van. Slowly she walked towards him, a small figure in fuchsia shorts and an oversized T-shirt, her black hair looped behind her ears, her feet bare and wet with dew.

He was wearing blue shorts and nothing else, the sun limning his body. Her breath caught in her throat. When she was within a few feet of him she held out the bouquet and said gravely, 'I've brought you a present.'

He took it from her, studying the innocent faces and naïve colours of the flowers. Then he smiled at her, a smile with no hidden meanings, a smile of simple pleasure in the beauty of the day. 'Breakfast is ready,' he said.

'You cooked breakfast?'

He nodded seriously. 'All by myself.'

She tested the air with her nose. 'Bacon? And coffee?'

'And blueberry pancakes.'

She wanted to say that, if he was not married, the women in Maine were crazy; but she was not sure she could carry off the remark with quite the necessary lightness of tone. 'Lead me to it,' she said instead.

Inside the van the bed had vanished, the couch once again in its place. Tyson had set the table with a blue-checked cloth and blue napkins, the china bone-white, the cream and sugar set blue-patterned pottery. Oddly touched, Roslin said, 'That looks so nice, Tyson. You went to a lot of trouble.'

He was getting a matching pottery vase for the flowers. His back to her, he said gruffly, 'A reaction to roughing it for so many years...help yourself to coffee.'

And ask no questions, she thought, filling two mugs from the percolator on the stove. Tyson put the flowers on the table, then served her with bacon and pancakes and passed the maple syrup. He helped himself, and before he sat down beside her on the couch he flicked the switch on the radio on the shelf. 'Hope you don't have an aversion to classical music?' he said as one of Handel's *concerti grossi* rollicked into the van.

Roslin stared hard at her pancakes. Her mother, a cellist of some renown, had loved that particular concerto. 'No, it's OK.'

'It's all I listen to,' Tyson rejoined with a note of underlying defiance, dousing his pancakes with syrup.

The bacon was crisp and the blueberries sweet. Feeling her way, Roslin said, 'You sound rather belligerent. Don't your friends like that kind of music?'

He grinned, a little-boy grin to which she could only grin back. 'I got in one of the worst—or the best, depending on your point of view—fights in my life over classical music.'

After stirring cream into his coffee he began eating, still with a half-smile on his lips. 'You can't stop there!' Roslin said indignantly.

'It's not a very edifying story.'

'Give, Tyson.'

'OK, OK…it happened when I was working in a nickel mine in the North-West Territories—I was only a kid, eighteen or nineteen. Twelve-hour shifts for six weeks at a time, pitch dark when you went to work and the same when you got off…so tempers got a little short, as you can imagine. There was one radio in the bunkhouse that could get the FM stations. One Thursday night Anton Kuerti was to play Beethoven—have you heard of Kuerti?'

She had met him in Los Angeles three years ago. 'Yes,' she said meekly.

'I let it be known I wanted to listen to that programme. But when the time came there was a country and western competition on one of the other channels and three of the guys decided that was more important than some—well, I'll use the word effeminate, although that wasn't the word they used—fellow in a funny coat tinkling away on a piano...these pancakes aren't bad, are they?'

'They're excellent. Don't change the subject, the suspense is killing me.'

'I felt I should assert myself,' Tyson said tranquilly. 'Three against one wasn't great odds, but I knew a trick or two that I'd picked up along the way and I figured I could at least make them reconsider their position on classical music. Be a little more broad-minded.' He chuckled. 'To cut the story short, I dusted the floor with them.'

'And how was Kuerti's concert?'

'I was afraid you'd ask that. Unfortunately, in the heat of battle, the radio got knocked off the shelf. Smashed into more pieces than notes in the concert. So no Kuerti. No country and western either, mind you.'

Roslin laughed outright. 'Kuerti would be flattered, I'm sure.' She glanced over at her companion. 'So you come by those muscles honestly. And the scars on your hands too, no doubt.'

'I got most of those working on an oil rig,' Tyson said briefly. 'My turn.' He touched her wrist. 'I noticed last night that you have very strong wrists and fingers—why is that?'

She was running away from everything that those wrists and fingers meant. She said awkwardly, 'I play indoor tennis. Are there any more pancakes?'

'Sure thing.'

Ashamed of herself for deceiving him, Roslin watched him get up and cross in front of the table to the stove. The sunlight coming through the windows slanted across his chest, the strong curve of his ribcage, and the flat belly. She had learned more about him this morning, she thought. That he had had a rough-and-tumble upbringing. That he was sensitive to the riches of music. Also that he made extremely good pancakes. She said impulsively, 'Tyson, can I be honest with you? I'm having a lot of trouble with the idea that you're going to drop me off at the main road and we'll never see each other again. Couldn't we at least exchange addresses? I promise I won't make a nuisance of myself.'

His movements very deliberate, he put a plate of pancakes on the table and topped up her coffee-mug. She stole a glance at his face. Impassive. Closed. Tense. She could guess what he was going to say before he said it.

'It's not a good idea, Roslin,' he replied heavily. 'Let me be equally honest. We're attracted to each other, not much sense in denying that. But you don't change lives on the basis of a passing sexual attraction, no matter how intense it seems at the time. I suppose the smartest thing would be to go to bed with each other and get it out of our system—but for all kinds of reasons we're not going to do that. So we'll do the next best thing— go our separate ways. Believe me, it's for the best.'

'You *are* married,' she whispered.

He drained his mug and thumped it on the table. 'Let's clean up the dishes.'

She could not handle working with him in the cramped space of the van. 'I'll do them, you cooked the meal. Why don't you go for a walk? You came here to get away from it all, didn't you?'

He must have heard the bitterness in her tone. His lips compressed. He said tightly, 'Is it all right if you get to Buckton around noon?'

She almost told him she was not going to Buckton, and consequently did not care if she ever got there. But why should she tell him where she would be living when he had no intentions of reciprocating? 'You don't have to take me to Buckton at all. The main highway will be fine, I can get a drive from there.'

'I am taking you to Buckton,' Tyson said, clipping off each word. 'It makes me shudder to think of you hitch-hiking...don't you ever read the papers?'

She said fliply, 'Only the funnies.'

'Grant me patience! Be ready to leave by ten-thirty, Roslin. I'll be back by then.' Shoving his feet in shabby sneakers, he jumped to the ground and set off towards the beach.

Roslin was not sorry to have the van to herself for an hour. At least if Tyson was at the beach she would not be tempted to seduce him, she thought with an unhappy twist of her mouth. If this was the way people felt for every passing attraction, no wonder the divorce rate was up. Was he right? Was the spark between them just a passing attraction and she too innocent to recognise it? Or was it something more, which he for his own reasons could not pursue?

She could not answer her own questions. But, after putting water on to heat for the dishes, she found herself checking the books on the shelf for an address and, when that did not succeed, trying the glove compartment for Tyson's registration forms.

The glove compartment was locked. With a sigh of frustration Roslin began clearing away the food. However, she did give herself the satisfaction of turning off the radio.

When Tyson came back the van was tidy, the floor swept and Roslin was sitting in the sun in her skirt and blouse, thin-strapped pink sandals on her feet, make-up on her face, her hair loosely knotted on the top of her head. 'Did you have a nice walk?' she asked politely.

She was not sure he heard her. His eyes fastened on her upturned face, he muttered, 'You're so incredibly beautiful...each time I see you it strikes me anew.'

'It's the Cover Girl look,' Roslin said flippantly. Then she glanced pointedly at her watch. 'Shouldn't we be leaving?'

For a moment he looked around him at the sun-drenched meadow alive with the songs of birds and the murmur of the waves, as though imprinting the scene on his memory against times when he might need it. 'I suppose we should.'

Steeling her heart against compassion, Roslin got to her feet. 'Your T-shirt's on the couch,' she said. She had wanted to bundle it up and stuff it in her backpack as a tangible reminder of an encounter whose inconclusiveness was already tearing her apart; only the thought that he might ask for it had stopped her.

Five minutes later they were bumping along the track towards Buck's ramshackle house. Buck was sprawled on the steps chewing a blade of grass; a young woman with red hair was shaking out a mat on the back porch. Tyson said drily, 'He's done it again—he sure must have sex appeal.'

'Or else there's an acute shortage of men on the Penisquit peninsula.'

Buck strolled over to the van, a ten-dollar bill changed hands, and Buck winked a bloodshot eye. 'Hope your night was as good as mine,' he drawled. 'You got a good eye for a woman, McCully, considerin' you don't hardly exercise it.'

'She can wash dishes, too,' Tyson remarked. 'See you, Buck.'

As he accelerated on to the road, Roslin snapped, 'That man is convinced we spent the night making mad, passionate love.'

'Well, we wanted to, didn't we?' Tyson said equably.

'Oh, be quiet!'

He took her at her word. The peaceful Maine countryside unfolded in front of them: rock-walled farms, marshes redolent with the tang of salt, gleaming inlets of the sea. Within an hour they had reached the highway that stretched from Calais to Kittery; Tyson turned right. Fifteen minutes later they passed the signposts for Carmel.

Great-Aunt Mellicent had been the sister of Roslin's maternal grandfather, with whom she had apparently quarrelled as a young woman; his portrait, repressive of mien, luxuriant of moustache, hung in the drawing-room of the house in Boston. Mellicent had never married, choosing to live in isolated splendour on a lonely peninsula in Maine, where she became mildly famous for her perennial gardens and for her interest in wildlife. She had not encouraged family visits. But six months ago Roslin had been informed by a firm of lawyers in Carmel that she was the main beneficiary of Great-Aunt Mellicent's will, and a week ago had been requested to inspect her newly acquired property. The final fight with Colby had taken place two days later, after which Roslin had taken to the roads, rich in acreage but with very little cash.

She found she was fretting as the van carried her farther and farther away from the signposts to Carmel. After waiting for six months, she did not want to wait any longer. Her whole future hung in the balance, she thought dramatically. If she hated the place, she would have to go back to the house in Boston. Back to Colby. Back to the piano. But if she liked it . . .

When a green and white signpost announced the town of Buckton, Tyson took the turn-off, following the directions to the main street. He pulled into a parking spot. 'Where do you want to go?' he said.

'Anywhere along here is fine.'

'Let me buy you lunch.'

'I'm not hungry,' Roslin said hastily, knowing she could not bear to sit in a crowded restaurant and make small talk with him.

'Have you got relatives here, somewhere to go?'

'I know where I'm going, yes.'

'That's not quite what I asked.' He undid his seat-belt and swivelled in the bucket seat so he was facing her. 'Roslin, I'm worried about you. I want to buy you a bus ticket back to Boston—I hate the thought of you hitching rides, it's not safe.'

'That's kind of you, Tyson, but no, thanks,' she said steadily, reaching down on the floor for her pack and looping it over one shoulder.

'You don't have much money, do you?'

'Enough.'

He fished in his pocket and took out a folded note. 'I want you to take——'

'Oh, Buck would love this,' she interrupted sarcastically.

'Buck's got nothing to do with it,' Tyson retorted. 'Use your common sense for a minute—you're broke and I'm not, and if you've got a bit of money you can stay in motels and take buses rather than exposing yourself to all kinds of dangers on the highway, and some day, when you're in a better position, you can pass the money on to someone else who needs it.' His smile was wintry. 'It's a loan, Roslin, that's all.'

'I can't take your money!'

His face closed. Slowly he replaced the folded note in his pocket. 'Then I guess this is goodbye.'

'I guess so.'

Her hand was on the door-latch. She glanced over at him, then wished she had not, for the clenched jaw muscles, the stormy grey eyes, echoed her own turmoil. But she had too much pride to plead her cause again. She said, 'Take care of yourself, Tyson,' stepped down to the pavement and shut the door. Briskly she set off along the street just as if she had a destination in mind, and in seconds was lost among the ambling crowds of tourists and summer residents. When she was certain she was out of sight, she ducked into the doorway of an antiques shop and looked back the way she had come.

The van was pulling out into the traffic. She tucked herself deeper into the alcove and watched it drive past. Tyson was staring straight ahead, his profile rigid, his hands locked on the wheel. A hundred yards ahead of her, he stopped at the traffic lights.

The licence plate, Roslin thought in panic. She had been so busy poking around the glove compartment that she had not done the obvious and copied down his plate numbers. Squeezing between two blue-rinsed matrons, nearly tripping over a whining child, she stumbled to the edge of the pavement and caught the flash of numbers as the van turned the corner. Her body sagged with relief, and she did not even notice how many curious stares she was attracting. She could trace him now. He was not lost to her forever.

She was in front of a delicatessen with a lunch bar. Going inside, Roslin ordered a bagel with cream cheese and bean sprouts, then sat at a table and wrote down the numbers. However, her brief euphoria had vanished. In a detective novel she would bribe an official to reveal Tyson's address and arrive triumphantly on his doorstep. But she was not a private investigator, and Tyson did not want to be found. If he had, he would have given her his address himself.

You can't cry in a public place, she adjured herself. You didn't cry at that dreadful competition in Budapest. So you won't cry now.

The bagel arrived. She chewed on it in a very concentrated way until the tightness in her throat eased. Then, at the table next to hers, she heard a man's voice mention the word Carmel. A couple were sitting there, in gaudy clothes that screamed Hawaii, devouring chocolate sundaes crowned with whipped cream, nuts, and cherries as brightly coloured as their shirts. They looked very safe.

'Excuse me,' Roslin said. 'I suppose you're not going to Carmel by any chance?'

'Sure thing,' said the husband.

'Take you there?' said the wife, who was gazing at Roslin's bean sprouts in aversion.

'I'd really appreciate that.'

'We're leaving as soon as we're finished here,' the wife went on comfortably. 'I should be eating what you're eating, dear, but I do love my desserts. And Fred,' she peeked archly at her husband, a most unromantic-looking man, 'loves me as I am, don't you, honey?'

'Sure thing,' said Fred.

So Roslin drove to Carmel, regaled with the pitfalls of vacations in Mexico, the Bahamas and Venezuela. 'No place like home, is there, dear?' said the wife, whose name was Gloria, as Fred stopped on Carmel's main street to let Roslin off.

Roslin managed to avoid answering this by thanking the two of them sincerely and wishing them a pleasant holiday. Then she looked around her.

Carmel breathed money. The stores had bow windows and gilt-edged signs, the lamp-posts must have marched right out of one of the ubiquitous antiques shops, the barrels of flowers that lined the pavement overflowed with lobelia and geraniums and alyssum. Even the trees planted at intervals along the street were groomed to an identical height and roundness. This manicured prettiness did not fit Roslin's image of Great-Aunt Mellicent. Frowning, she searched for the lawyer's name among the gilt.

Cuthbertson and Smith, between a jeweller's and a furriers, boasted leaded glass and blindingly polished brass. As Roslin walked in, a bell chimed and a secretary as manicured as the main street said, 'May I help you?' managing in the simple query to convey her disdain for Roslin's skirt and blouse.

'I'm looking for William Smith,' Roslin said placidly.

'One moment, please. I'll get him.'

William Smith did not even notice what Roslin was wearing. He was perhaps twenty-five, his red hair ruthlessly clipped, his summerweight suit out of the pages of a preppy magazine; he was gazing at Roslin with a dazzlement of which his senior partner would scarcely have approved. Certainly the secretary did not. 'Miss

Hebb? Delighted to meet you,' he said, and pressed her hand with unlegal fervour.

Reclaiming her fingers, she responded, 'I've come to see my property.'

'Of course, of course, I'll get the keys and we'll go right now. A lovely day for an outing; how fortunate that the fog stayed offshore.'

Two minutes later Roslin was being ushered into a silver BMW, where she asked the one question that had been worrying her. 'May I take possession of the property immediately, Mr Smith?'

'Please call me William,' he said with an engaging grin that Roslin decided he probably practised in front of the mirror. 'Most certainly you may. Although of course you'll want to put it on the market as soon as possible; this is a prime time for selling shore properties.'

She stifled several retorts and said amicably, 'We'll see.'

'You'd be very foolish not to,' he reproved her. 'I have at least two potential buyers lined up for you. Although, of course, Carmel will be the loser when you move on,' he added gallantly.

He reminded her of a puppy whose obedience-school training had not quite taken. '*I* shall decide whether or not to sell, Mr Smith,' she said, and gave him her most brilliant smile.

Not noticeably subdued, he pointed out some of the sights of Carmel, including a whole series of stately mansions in parklike surroundings. Roslin did not think she would care to live with neo-Georgian stone or Greek columns; neither did starkly angled cedar appeal. Her heart was thumping in her breast by the time William Smith said, 'We're nearly there.'

The BMW was purring down a country road edged with lush trees. Then the road descended to a narrow isthmus with an expanse of marsh on one side and a sandy beach on the other. 'The property begins here,' said the lawyer, 'and takes in the whole peninsula. You own the marsh, the beach and approximately sixty more acres...you'll find the grounds in pretty good condition.'

Later Roslin was to remember his slight emphasis on the word 'grounds'. But they were climbing the hill of the peninsula proper, so her attention was wholly on the scenery. The trees were magnificent: venerable oaks, wineglass elms, spreading maples, all set in overgrown grass. Then banks of rhododendrons and a tangle of other shrubbery replaced the trees, and the garden came into view, terraced to fit the landscape, a blaze of colour. 'Miss Cowper's life revolved around that garden,' William Smith said with not so much disapproval as incomprehension.

But once again Roslin did not reply, for by now the house was in sight. She let out her breath in a long sigh. It was perfect.

It was a simple one-and-a-half-storey salt-box painted pale green with bottle-green trim, the square-paned windows twinkling in the sun, the brick chimney speaking of winter evenings around the fireplace. 'Dry rot,' said William Smith.

'I beg your pardon,' said Roslin.

'Dry rot in the attic, the roof leaks, and part of the foundation is giving way. The whole place should be levelled to the ground. As I said, your great-aunt spent all her time—and money—on the gardens.'

Roslin said carefully, 'I get the impression you did not care for my great-aunt.'

'No, no, not at all. But the sensible thing for her to have done years ago was to sell this place—there was no shortage of buyers—and move into a senior citizens' home. A very superior one,' he finished meaningfully, turning off the engine and getting out of the car.

Roslin got out as well. In the drowsy heat of a July afternoon the birds were largely silent and the wind no more than a whisper through the trees; the air was saturated with the scent of roses and honeysuckle. She said calmly, 'May I have the keys to the house, please, Mr

Smith? I'd like to go through it on my own, if you don't mind.'

'But I should——'

'Please.'

'I'll wait for you out here,' he said stiffly, and passed her the key-ring. 'You'll soon see what I mean about the state of the house.'

Ignoring him, Roslin crossed the driveway and walked up the stone path to the front door of the house. Her house.

It was cool inside and very quiet. It was also shabby and not overly clean. But the furniture was solid and the chintz fabrics had faded pleasantly and the sunlight poured through the windows. Like a woman in a trance Roslin went from room to room, climbing the creaking stairs, admiring the sloping roofs of the bedrooms that were tucked under the eaves, loving the worn pine floors and the delicate wallpapers. The only source of discord was her discovery of an old grand piano in a room at the back of the house; there was a key in the door and on impulse she locked the door, wrestled with the nearest window until it squealed open, and threw the key as far as she could. It landed in the middle of a thicket of rosebushes.

After closing the window and dusting off her hands, she went downstairs, letting herself out of the back door. In the shed behind the house she found, among a huge array of garden tools, a bicycle in working order. She had all she needed.

William Smith was leaning against his car looking thoroughly bored; not for him the pleasures of horticulture, Roslin thought mischievously, and she called out, 'I love the house—you can leave me here if you like.'

He looked at her as if she had gone mad. 'Aren't you staying at the inn in town?'

One night at an inn in Carmel could totally wreck her budget. 'I'm going to stay here,' she said cheerfully.

'By yourself?'

'That's the general idea.'

'I see,' he said, a patent lie. Then he ran a finger around his collar. 'I'm not sure I can round up either of my prospective buyers this afternoon...one's a developer from Buckton, the other's a local man who, rumour has it, is to be married soon. But I could certainly have them here some time tomorrow.'

'I don't want to sell, Mr Smith.'

He said pompously, 'Miss Hebb, as your lawyer I would be doing you a grave disservice to keep you in ignorance as to the potential value of your inheritance. I see it as my duty to at least allow you to meet these men and discuss the situation thoroughly.'

When Colby spoke that way, Roslin had learned not to argue; it was a waste of time. 'Very well,' she said. 'But in all fairness you should tell them before they come that I am not interested in selling.'

William Smith did not look quite as enchanted with her as he had earlier. 'The telephone and power bills have been paid out of the estate—which as you know is minimal apart from the property—until the end of the month. After that they are your responsibility. My personal phone number is in the book should you have any questions, Miss Hebb.' He gave her a formal bow. 'Good afternoon.'

Roslin was smiling as she watched his car disappear from sight. Freedom, she thought. The whole place was hers. She was accountable to no one. She did a solemn little dance in the middle of the driveway, then went inside to make up a grocery list.

CHAPTER FOUR

THAT afternoon Roslin bicycled to a country store about a mile from the house, buying cleaning supplies and enough food for two days. She phoned Mrs Granmont, the housekeeper in Boston, and asked her to forward the trunk that had been packed for the last week. Then she set out to explore the peninsula. There was another small beach on the far side; there were coves and inlets where seaweed swayed in the water; there were innumerable birds and a family of muskrats and a bewildering assortment of trees. And around the house there were the glorious hues of the flowerbeds.

Roslin knew a little about gardening from her mother. After a light supper, she weeded happily for two hours. Then she went inside, had a bath and went to bed in the room that overlooked the marshes. Firmly shutting her mind against any memories of Tyson, filling it instead with plans for the next day, she went to sleep.

She slept soundly, got up early, and by eleven o'clock had the living-room vacuumed, the furniture and the oak floor gleaming, the windows open to the summer air. Taking scissors, she went outside to pick some flowers. Again she felt very happy; she loved both house and garden, and they were proving the perfect cure for that unsatisfactory episode with Tyson.

She was walking back to the house, her arms full of day lilies, bellflowers, daisies and bee balm, when she heard a car approaching. William Smith, she thought crossly. She was about to be taught the value of her inheritance.

She disliked the man William had brought immediately and intensely. He was too perfectly groomed, too cold-eyed; he was also unhealthily overweight. He was like Carmel, she thought unfairly. Worth a lot of money and determined everyone should know it.

'Good morning, Roslin,' William said, trying not to stare too obviously at her bare legs. 'I'd like you to meet Bradleigh Waldron, he's a property developer from Buckton.'

The armful of flowers meant Roslin did not have to shake hands. She smiled insincerely and said, 'I expect Mr Smith has explained that I don't want to sell the property, Mr Waldron.'

'Indeed he has. Yes, indeed. Yet I felt a meeting between us would be to our mutual advantage, Miss Hebb...I have great plans for this peninsula, great plans.' He rubbed his hands together; his diamond rings were ostentatious to the point of vulgarity. 'Perhaps we could go inside to discuss them?'

The flowers were heavy and an ant was crawling up her arm; yet Roslin did not want her first visitors to be a lawyer and a land developer. 'Why don't we sit outside?' she suggested, leading them to two stone benches that overlooked the garden.

Bradleigh Waldron brushed off the bench before sitting down. He looked around him in a businesslike way. 'The first step would be to fill in the marsh, it only breeds flies. Then I'll subdivide into four fifteen-acre lots, each with an architecturally designed dwelling...these will be desirable and important properties, Miss Hebb, indeed, yes.'

'And the house?' she said non-committally.

He gestured with one hand. 'The house is nothing. Raze it to the ground. A few trees would have to go, of course. But I'd keep most of them, they add to the value immeasurably.'

'They're also beautiful,' Roslin remarked.

'Yes, yes.' He leaned forward confidentially. 'I'm prepared to make you a very generous offer, Miss Hebb. Very generous indeed.' He named a sum which made her blink, and continued, 'We could settle as soon as possible, I'd like to get started right away. Cash outright, Miss Hebb...that's my policy.'

She almost expected him to pull the notes from his pocket; with a pang she thought of Tyson offering her money because he was worried about her. She said impatiently, 'But I don't want to sell, Mr Waldron.'

The smile vanished. 'I might be able to go a little higher,' he said. 'But not much, Miss Hebb. Not much.'

'I'm not being difficult to try and raise the price,' she said coldly. 'I am simply telling the truth—I don't want to sell.' Especially to the likes of you, she added to herself.

His amiability vanished. He named another figure, higher than the first, adding curtly, 'That's my final offer. Why don't you think it over? I'm sure you'll find it's to your advantage to sell, Miss Hebb.'

With what in a woman would have been called a flounce he got up from the bench and marched across the grass to the car, signalling to William to follow him. But when he reached the BMW he turned so suddenly that Roslin jumped. His eyes flat as a reptile's, his ponderous body full of menace, he said softly, 'I do urge you to consider my offer very seriously, Miss Hebb. This really is not an ideal place for a young woman to live alone. Not another house in sight—have you noticed that?'

Then he gestured impatiently at the hapless William. 'We'll have to hurry, I have another appointment,' he snapped, and squeezed himself into the front seat. William waved at her with an eloquent shrug of his shoulders and drove away.

Under the hot sun Roslin felt her skin creep with cold. She looked around. The developer was right. There were no other houses in sight. She was alone in a pastoral landscape that half an hour ago had breathed serenity and the joys of freedom.

It was the same landscape, she thought sturdily. No reason to feel afraid. Bradleigh Waldron might be a man whose values were the antithesis of hers, but if she chose not to sell he could do nothing to make her change her mind. Nothing.

Nevertheless her nerves were on edge as she arranged the flowers in crystal vases and carried them into the living-room, and although she had planned to sunbathe after lunch she felt the need for some kind of energetic activity to erase the nasty little encounter with the land developer. The kitchen, she thought. She would tackle the kitchen.

Great-Aunt Mellicent might have been a marvellous gardener, but she had been a lousy housekeeper, Roslin decided, filling a pail at the stained sink whose taps were encrusted with grime. The kitchen was filthy. No other word for it. Opening the window to let in the scent of wallflowers, she sprayed the oven with cleaning compound, and started washing out the cupboards.

Two hours later she was coming to the conclusion that the oven cleaner was over-rated. She had seen all the TV commercials of smiling women in pretty dresses merrily wiping the insides of their ovens; she would have liked to have had one of them here right now. Great-Aunt Mellicent's oven would make them change their tune. Grunting to herself, she scrubbed away with the steel wool.

'Miss Hebb,' William Smith's voice said tentatively from behind her. 'Did you forget I was coming back?'

Roslin dropped the steel wool, banged her head on the roof of the oven, and looked up. The lawyer was standing at the kitchen door. Behind him was Tyson McCully.

Her mouth fell open. *'You!'* she gasped.

'You own this house?' Tyson snapped back.

William looked from one to the other. 'You know each other?'

Roslin stayed crouched on the floor, because she had all too clear a mental picture of what she must look like, and the less of her that showed, the better. Earlier she had pinned her braid on top of her head, but her exertions had caused it to fall down and the ends were daubed with oven cleaner. As was a fair proportion of the rest of her. She said icily, 'You didn't tell me you lived in Carmel.'

'You didn't tell me you were coming here. What did you do, hitch-hike from Buckton right after I left?'

He looked extremely angry. 'Yes,' she said. 'That's precisely what I did.'

He stepped round William, who seemed to have lost his voice, picked up a piece of paper towel and rubbed her cheekbone. 'It's the oven you're supposed to be cleaning,' he said.

The grey eyes that she remembered so well were as stormy as when he had said goodbye to her. Forever, she thought with a quiver of laughter, and felt him take her by the elbow and lift her to her feet. Her shorts were skimpy, her tank top revealed more of her cleavage than was discreet, and her cheeks, she was sure, were scarlet. Trying to collect her wits, she said in a voice that was intended to sound efficient but merely sounded peevish, 'I'm not selling—didn't William tell you that?'

From the doorway William interposed, 'Mr McCully would not be developing the property at all—simply tearing down the house and rebuilding.'

'How nice,' Roslin retorted. 'You're the second person today who wants to tear down my house, Tyson McCully. *My* house. Note the personal pronoun.'

'Who else was here?' Tyson demanded.

'A thoroughly unpleasant character by the name of Bradleigh Waldron. He plans to fill in the marsh. Do you plan to fill in the marsh, Tyson?'

'Bradleigh would bulldoze his mother's grave if he thought it would make him a dollar. Don't sell to him, Roslin, for goodness' sake.'

Exasperated, she said, 'I'm not selling to anyone. *Anyone.* Got that?' Quite suddenly she remembered something William had said. Her eyes narrowed. 'Are you getting married?'

'Who told you that?'

William said weakly, 'I may have mentioned——'

'Out!' Tyson yelled so loudly that Roslin backed into the oven door. 'Miss Hebb and I will discuss a fair price for this heap of dry rot and crumbling bricks, William, and then we will meet you outside.'

William left. So would Roslin under similar circumstances. She said irritably, 'There's no need to raise your voice, we're not deaf. You're the one who's behaving as though you're deaf, Tyson. I don't want to sell my house. Everyone is taking great pains to point out the dry rot, the decrepitude of the basement, and the leaks in the roof—it doesn't make a bit of difference. I like the house. I love the house. I am planning to live in the house. Do you understand?' She scowled. 'And who are you marrying, anyway?'

'As far as I am aware, in all my thirty years I have yet to propose to anyone.'

'William thinks you're getting married.'

'I've been dating someone for five or six months,' he said shortly.

Bradleigh had brought one kind of menace, Tyson another; again Roslin felt cold. 'She's the reason you wouldn't give me your address.'

Tyson moved his shoulders as if his shirt was too tight. 'I suppose so.'

She looked up at him. Have you slept with her? she wanted to ask. Have you made love to her? 'She's the reason you took off in the van by yourself. You needed to get away from her.'

'Roslin, you don't know the first thing about me and Liza... so will you kindly mind your own business?'

Her stomach was churning. She had discovered something about herself in the past few seconds: that she could not bear to think of Tyson in another woman's arms. Which in theory was indeed none of her business.

Although he was wearing light trousers and a blazer, perfectly correct clothes in which, she had to admit, he looked very handsome, the kitchen seemed too cramped to contain him; again she had that sense of fierce energy only just under control. Without thinking, she said, 'I can't picture you in Carmel—it's too small for you, too prim and proper. What on earth do you do here—besides date Liza?' she finished with a grimace.

'I could ask exactly the same of you. You're not really planning to live here, are you?'

'All by myself,' she said pertly.

'Then I hope you've got lots of money. Were you hitch-hiking because you get your kicks that way, or because you didn't have the money for the bus?'

Unerringly he had found her vulnerable spot. Nine months from now, when Roslin turned twenty-one, Colby would pass over her trust fund and she would have her parents' money. But until then, apart from a small monthly allowance, she had very little in the way of ready cash. She said flatly, '*That's* none of *your* business.'

He moved away from her, looking out of the window at the dusky wallflowers whose scent was defeated by the acrid odour of oven cleaner. 'Will you show me the rest of the house?'

'No. What's the point?'

'But William was unwise enough to promise me a showing...so I guess I'll just have to look on my own, won't I?' Giving her a wolfish smile, he left the kitchen.

She could run after him, waving the can of oven cleaner. Or she could preserve her dignity and wait for him to come back. Under no illusions that she could stop him whatever she did, Roslin settled for the latter course and knelt on the floor again, brandishing the steel wool as if Tyson were on the receiving end.

By the time he came back the oven was almost finished. He leaned against the doorframe, and for a moment he was the man who had sat beside her in friendship at the breakfast table in the van. 'I can see why you like the house,' he said.

She smiled at him, quite willing for a truce. 'It welcomed me the first time I saw it.'

'What's in the room upstairs that's locked?'

Her lashes flickered. She inserted one of the racks in the oven and said vaguely, 'The key seems to be missing.'

'Roslin, you can't live here alone. A five-year-old could pick the lock on the back door or climb in one of the windows.'

She stood up, wishing she were taller, and said very quietly, 'Don't tell me what to do, Tyson.'

'I want this place and I'm willing to pay for it.' The sum he mentioned was more than Bradleigh's second offer. 'Cleaning the oven won't stop the rain coming in the roof. You'd have to spend a fortune in repairs to make the house habitable and you haven't got that kind of money, Roslin, I know you haven't. I want the place. You can't afford to keep it. So sell it to me. It's very simple.'

His logic was impeccable. She said, 'And what of my feelings, Tyson? I haven't had a proper home in six years, and this house felt like home as soon as I walked in the door. I can be free here, I can be myself; I need this house... what of that?'

His eyes were bleak. 'You can't live on sentiment, I learned that a long time ago.'

She forgot about the oven, Liza, and her problematical property in a swift surge of compassion. Crossing the room, she looked straight into his eyes and said, 'Not sentiment, Tyson...emotions. Feelings. There's a world of difference.'

'Is there?' With one hand he traced the curve of her collarbone. Then, with an inarticulate groan, he took her in his arms and kissed her.

His lips burned through all her defences to the woman within, and despite her inexperience she matched his passion with a passion of her own, instinctively arching

her neck as his mouth trailed her throat, shuddering as
he crushed the softness of her breasts. Then he pushed
her away, his chest heaving. 'I suppose you'd call that
emotion, would you, Roslin? Well, it's not. Not in my
books. Call it sex or lust or desire, or all three—but not
emotion.'

'Then why are you so angry?' she blazed. .

'Because I knew where I was until you came along,'
he snarled. 'I said goodbye to you yesterday because I
thought it was the best thing to do. You're a sea-witch
who's cast a spell on me and I don't run my life that
way; you could turn everything upside-down and I won't
allow that, do you hear me?'

'I shouldn't be surprised if William can hear you!'

He swore under his breath. 'Sell me the house,
Roslin—you've got no choice. Then get out of Carmel.'

If she had had doubts before, she had none now. 'No,'
she said.

'You think I'm playing games, don't you? I'm not—
this is for real. Bradleigh is a dangerous and unscrupu-
lous man, who by a certain native cunning and the right
connections has managed to stay on the right side of the
law. He wants this place. If I buy it, I can handle
Bradleigh . . . in fact, I'd enjoy the opportunity. But you
can't. Not on your own.'

Step by step Tyson was destroying her peace of mind
and the precious, healing serenity of Great-Aunt
Mellicent's inheritance. Roslin said furiously, 'I hate
what you're doing to me—go away, Tyson, and don't
come back!'

She stamped out of the kitchen, through the hall, and
flung open the front door, her eyes glittering like the
panes of antique glass inset around the door. Tyson was
at her heels. He took her by the elbow, said in a staccato
voice, 'I'm going to buy this place and you're not going
to stand in my way,' and strode across the gravel to the
BMW. This time Roslin did not wait to see if William
waved. She slammed the door, went through her entire

repertoire of swear-words, which unfortunately was not nearly extensive enough to do justice to her feelings, and stormed back to the kitchen.

At seven o'clock that evening the front doorbell rang. Roslin had put her anger to good use: the kitchen sparkled, and the wallflowers were finally conquering the combined smells of ammonia and floor wax. She had had a bath afterwards and was sitting in the living-room with a sandwich and a cup of tea when she heard the crunch of footsteps and then the peal of the bell. Bradleigh? William? Tyson? Bracing herself, she opened the door.

Two elderly ladies stood on the step, one with cherries on her hat, the other with poppies. Otherwise they appeared to be identical. 'Hello,' said Roslin.

'I'm Amy Prestwick and this is my friend Annabel Westhaver. We heard you'd moved in and we wanted to welcome you to the neighbourhood,' said the poppy lady. 'We were friends of your dear aunt's.'

'You mean you don't want to buy the place?' Roslin blurted.

'Goodness me, no, why would we want to do that? We have places of our own, don't we, Amy?' said the wearer of the cherries.

'Very nice places,' said Amy. 'We walked up, as it's such a lovely evening.'

Belatedly recalling her manners, and very glad she had cleaned the living-room, Roslin ushered them in. 'Please sit down, you're my first proper visitors. May I get you a cup of tea?'

A few minutes later, when they were settled with tea and biscuits, Amy said, 'You don't look much like your aunt, dear.'

'My great-aunt, actually. Tell me about her; I only recall meeting her once when I was very young.'

She could almost see their faces light up at the prospect of a good gossip. As they chattered away Roslin gained a picture of an intelligent, self-sufficient woman who would brook no nonsense, yet who would make a very loyal friend. 'It was she who got us interested in birds, dear,' said Amy. 'We're both members of the local bird society. This property is quite famous in a small way, you see, because migratory shorebirds stop off in the marsh; we're right on their route.'

'Oh,' said Roslin. 'A man called Bradleigh Waldron called here today; he wants to subdivide the property and fill in the marsh.'

Amy's cheeks went pink. 'He's not a nice man, dear.'

Annabel said, 'He doesn't care about the bitterns and the plovers.'

'He only wants to make money,' Amy sniffed.

'We do hope you won't sell to him, dear.'

'Mellicent would be so upset.'

Suppressing a vision of her great-aunt's ghost chasing her with a garden fork, Roslin said, 'I want to live here myself.' She hesitated. 'Tyson McCully wants to buy it, too.'

'Dear me,' said Annabel.

'He must be going to marry Liza, then,' Amy remarked.

'Such a waste.'

'She is your great-niece, Annabel.'

'I never really cared for her, though.'

'I do admit she doesn't seem quite the right woman for Tyson,' Amy concluded with a decisive nod of the poppies.

Roslin finally managed to get a word in. 'You know Tyson?'

'Since he was born. Such a sweet baby, despite that dreadful father of his.'

'And his mother...' Annabel sighed, giving her friend a meaningful look. 'But we mustn't speak ill of the dead, must we, Amy?'

'We shouldn't, no,' Amy agreed, rather wistfully.

Roslin could have screamed. 'I didn't realise he came from here,' she said casually.

'Oh, yes,' Amy said. 'But he was away for years.'

'He came back six months ago.'

'Which is when Liza came back, too.'

'After her divorce.'

'Quite a coincidence, really.' Amy sighed, then brightened perceptibly. 'So you've met Tyson, dear?'

'What did you think of him?' Annabel asked.

They looked like two little birds themselves, anxiously waiting for crumbs. Roslin said with careful truth, 'He's a very forceful man.'

'He's had to be, dear.'

Annabel cocked her head. 'But handsome, wouldn't you agree?'

Two pairs of eyes were fastened on her face. Roslin fought down a tendency to blush and said sternly, 'Handsome is as handsome does.'

Shocked, Amy said, 'Tyson isn't like Bradleigh.'

'How those two used to fight as boys!' said Annabel.

'Tyson is straight,' Amy finished, not to be deflected.

Roslin said blandly, 'I'm glad to hear it. He wasn't very happy when I wouldn't sell the house.'

'I'm glad you won't sell it to him. We wouldn't want to encourage anything, would we?' said Amy. 'Well, we must go, dear. It's been so nice meeting you.'

'You must come and visit us,' Annabel added.

'The first two cottages after the store.'

'Even though we've known each other all our lives, we've never lived together, you see.'

'That's why we've stayed such good friends.'

Amy and Annabel smiled at each other and then at Roslin and made their farewells. Roslin watched them set off down the drive, greatly cheered by her two new acquaintances. They were very sweet. They did not want to buy her house. And they did not think Liza was the woman for Tyson.

*   *   *

Roslin slept well, despite Bradleigh's veiled threats and Tyson's not so veiled warnings, and woke again to sunshine. She schooled herself to clean the bathroom and the front hall that morning, taking great pleasure in hanging curtains on the clothes-line behind the house and shaking years of dust from the old Persian rugs. But after lunch she went out into the garden. Wearing her jeans, and a large shirt she had found in her great-aunt's closet, and armed with pruning shears, she began cutting the dead wood from the clumps of Rugosa roses that flourished near the shed. She sang as she worked.

She knew her euphoria was not related totally to either housewifery or horticulture. Tyson lived in Carmel; he had not vanished from her life. Tyson had compared her to a sea-witch.

A sea-witch seemed more romantic than an almost-fiancée. And, if he was as straight as Amy had insisted, surely he wouldn't kiss Liza with the same passion with which he had kissed her? Humming to herself, she tugged a long sucker free of the bush.

'Excuse me,' said a cool, well-bred voice. 'I'm looking for Roslin Hebb.'

The sucker snagged Roslin's sleeve, the thorns scratching her arm. She twisted around, still entangled, knowing intuitively whom she was about to meet. A guest-book was what she needed, she thought, and smiled cautiously at her visitor. 'I'm Roslin.'

There was a moment's silence as the other woman assessed her. Then the well-bred voice said, 'How do you do? I'm Liza Westhaver.'

A vicious yank liberated Roslin from the sucker. 'Shall we go inside?' she said politely, trying not to stare.

Liza Westhaver was beautiful in a manner as cool and well-bred as her voice. Her casual sportswear, her cap of blonde hair and her make-up were more Laura Ashley than *Vogue*; she had the unconscious arrogance and the perfect teeth of one who has never had to worry about money. She said, 'I don't think that will be necessary.'

So this was not a social call. Roslin pulled off her work gloves and dropped them on the ground. 'Let's sit on the benches in front of the house,' she suggested, adding limpidly, 'I love the view.'

She led the way round the house, hoping Liza was recognising the curtains belling on the line as a sign of permanent occupancy, and offered Liza the bench on which Bradleigh had lowered his considerable bulk. Sitting down herself, she said, 'Do you like gardening, Miss Westhaver?'

Liza did not bother answering. 'I want you to sell your property to Tyson McCully, Miss Hebb.'

'I thought you might want to buy it yourself—along with everyone else in Carmel,' Roslin responded.

'No,' Liza said composedly. 'Tyson wants it, and I want Tyson to have it.'

'My only objection is that I want it, too.'

'You can't possibly live here on your own.'

'So people keep telling me.' Roslin plucked a weed from the grass. 'So far it's working very well.'

'The house is falling down and the grounds need a tremendous amount of upkeep,' Liza said, her cheeks growing pink.

'I certainly would like to maintain the gardens in some kind of order. But if the weeds take over the rest of the property it won't really matter...all the better for the birds.'

'You've been talking to Amy and Annabel!'

'They were kind enough to welcome me to the neighborhood last night, yes.' Roslin gave her companion an innocent smile.

Liza raised her chin; she had herself under control again. 'I think you're being purposely obstructive, Miss Hebb. Presumably you're trying to get more money out of Tyson——'

Smoothly Roslin interrupted. 'Which is, I would have thought, Tyson's concern rather than yours.' With a curiosity too strong for her own liking, she added, 'Does he know you're here?'

'Tyson and I are very close—his concerns are mine.'

'In that case, you can give him a message from me. Tell him I am no more interested in selling the property today than I was yesterday. Or I will be tomorrow.' Roslin got up from the bench. 'Now I'd better get back to the rose-bushes . . . we wouldn't want the place to get run down, would we, Miss Westhaver?'

Liza also stood up. She said imperiously, 'I don't think you quite understand . . . I *want* Tyson to have this property.'

Rather ashamed of her sarcasm, Roslin said quietly, 'But we don't always get what we want.'

'I see no reason why I should not in this particular case.' Liza gave her a frosty smile. 'I'd hoped I could make you see reason. I was wrong. Goodbye, Miss Hebb.'

Roslin did not bother saying goodbye. She trailed back to the rose-bushes, but her pleasure in the task seemed to have gone. She might have scored points in that verbal battle, but she felt like the loser. If Liza was the kind of woman Tyson would marry then she, Roslin, had gravely misjudged him. And, if Liza and Tyson were to be living as man and wife in Carmel, Great-Aunt Mellicent's property would lose much of its appeal.

Rationally this did not make sense. But the heaviness of Roslin's heart told her it was so.

CHAPTER FIVE

FOR three days Roslin did not have a single visitor. She threw herself into the house-cleaning, for it was one way of putting her seal on the house, confirming her sense of ownership, and she finished the downstairs and two of the bedrooms. She did not attempt to open the room with the piano, even though at some deep level she was acutely missing the music around which her life had revolved for so many years. She was not consciously ready to admit she missed it; and whenever a melody or a phrase echoed in her mind she did her best to ignore it.

Her trunk arrived from Boston, giving her a far greater variety of clothes and enabling her to place some of her personal effects around the house. Her books, modern paperbacks, mixed uneasily with her great-aunt's staid, leatherbound sets of Dickens and Kipling. But the photos of her parents looked very much at home on the mantel in the living-room.

On the third day she cycled into Carmel. Her first stop was the bank, a hexagonal brick building adorned with columns and big double doors and topped by a weather vane. She asked for the manager, was ushered into his office and read the gold-lettered sign on his desk with a sinking heart. Frederick Westhaver, it said.

Frederick Westhaver had the same pale blue eyes as Liza, with much the same lack of expression in them. Calmly Roslin stated the purpose of her visit, which was to arrange a loan with her trust fund as collateral in order that she have the money to pay the taxes and make some repairs, and just as calmly heard him refuse. His reasons were fluent and no doubt well-rehearsed. Liza, she realised without surprise, had reached him first.

She went outside into the sunshine, which seemed to be a permanent fixture in Carmel, and unlocked her bicycle. She would have to get in touch with the trustees in Boston, and hope that Colby had not thwarted her there as Liza had here. She was rather surprised she had not heard from her uncle. Surprised, and uneasy. Silence from Colby usually meant he was up to something.

She bought groceries, did not see either Tyson or Liza, and pedalled home. But when she tried to reach the head trustee, a man she had always liked, she discovered he was out of the office for two days. It did not really matter, Roslin told herself firmly. Her allowance was adequate to cover day-to-day expenses, and the repairs could wait.

However, she was left prey to a nasty, niggling suspicion. Had Liza spoken to the bank manager? Or had Tyson? She had expected to see Tyson before this. She had certainly not expected him to give up so easily.

She got rid of some of her unease by weeding the perennial borders that flanked the house, and that evening watched British comedies on the black and white television set in the living-room. Refusing to acknowledge that she was lonely, or that she would have liked someone with whom to share the jokes—Tyson?—she went to bed early.

She woke in the middle of the night from a confused dream in which she was in a sail-boat that was taking in water faster than she could bail it out. Liza had been sitting in the bow, watching her. Smirking, if someone as well-bred as Liza could be said to smirk. Hastily Roslin sat up.

Rain was drumming on the roof and rattling against the windowpanes. She had left one window open, and the curtain was slapping wetly on the glass.

She got out of bed and hurried to the window. But before closing it she looked out for a moment. She could see nothing but a black, impenetrable darkness. Not another house in sight.

Shivering, she latched the window shut and went into the bathroom for paper towel to wipe the floor. Then, over the relentless rhythm of the rain she heard another sound, a steady drip, drip, drip. It was coming from the far end of the hall. She switched on the light.

Water was welling through the ceiling and splashing in a large puddle on the floor. The floor that she had waxed only yesterday. She ran downstairs to get a pail and cloths, and from the dining-room heard the same ominous splashing. The rest of the night Roslin spent scurrying from room to room, for as the rain persisted the leaks proliferated, and the yellowed stains she had noticed in the ceilings when she was cleaning explained themselves. At dawn the rain lessened. She emptied all the buckets, collapsed into bed and fell asleep. When she awoke mid-morning, two of the buckets had overflowed. Her lips compressed, she cleaned up the mess.

By the middle of the afternoon Roslin was both exhausted and deeply discouraged. Tyson was right. She could not stay here. If the roof leaked this badly in a summer rainsquall, what would it do under a foot of snow? And how was she to get back and forth to the shops in winter without a car? Even today she was isolated, for it was no day to go anywhere by bike.

She could not afford a car. She certainly could not afford to fix the roof. She didn't even have enough money to pay the taxes. Great-Aunt Mellicent, no doubt with the best of intentions, had left her a white elephant. She wanted very badly to put her head down on the arm of the chesterfield and cry her eyes out. But that, she thought with a wry twist of her mouth, would only add to the humidity. Not an advisable course of action. Anyway, it was time to empty the buckets again.

By evening Roslin was feeling more cheerful. The radio had assured her of clear skies tonight and sunshine tomorrow, and the dripping was now adagio rather than prestissimo. Re-energised, she decided to try out the fireplace.

After placing logs on top of carefully arranged kindling and newspaper, she put a match to the paper. Little yellow flames licked at the blackened edges and blue smoke spiralled upwards. Roslin sat back on her heels. A fire was very basic, she reflected. Cavemen had cooked over fires. But they had also used them to keep the darkness at bay. The effect was psychological as much as physical . . . at which point her profundities were interrupted by a puff of smoke in her face.

She coughed and waved her hands to dissipate it. But the smoke was now pouring out of the fireplace in thick clouds as the flames crackled among the kindling. Rubbing her eyes, she tried to peer up the chimney. Smoke was supposed to go up chimneys, everyone knew that. Why was this smoke contravening all the principles of physics?

Coughing and hacking, she ran to the kitchen, where it seemed a supreme irony that she should have to fill a bucket with water. Trying not to spill any, she lugged the bucket back to the living-room and threw the water on the fire.

The fireplace belched smoke and steam. Kneeling down, Roslin beat out the last of the flames with the poker, trying not to breathe, her eyes running. The hiss of steam gradually subsided, and into the silence the doorbell chimed.

She dropped the poker with a clatter, her heart thumping. Amy and Annabel would not venture out on a night like this. Nor would Liza. Was it a return visit from Bradleigh? For a moment she eyed the poker, almost tempted to take it with her. Then, chiding herself for being a fool, she marched to the front door and pulled it open. Tyson was standing on the step.

Roslin discovered she was glad to see him. Not just glad. Delighted. Happy. Ecstatic. Trying to smother a silly grin, she said, 'Come in.'

He handed her his trench coat, in which he put James Bond to shame, and said, 'Why is it that every time I see you you're either soaking wet or very dirty?'

There was a mirror in the hall, with gilt cherubs simpering at the four corners. Roslin regarded herself in silence. Her face was streaked with soot, her shirt splattered with ashes, and as usual her hair seemed to be falling down. With a certain satisfaction she concluded that she looked as different from Liza as it was possible to look. 'Next time you call I'll be reclining on the couch in my caftan. Crocheting,' she added thoughtfully.

'I doubt it,' was the dry response. Then he tested the air with his nose. 'What are you doing, burning the house down instead of selling it?'

'The chimney's plugged.'

'I see.' His eyes were very watchful. 'And how did you fare in all the rain, Roslin?'

'I thought I might apply for a job with the local fire department,' she said dulcetly. 'I'm a mean hand with a bucket.'

The hall was narrow, and she was sure laughter briefly gleamed in his face. However, he said repressively, 'You're not a stupid woman—you must have realised you can't possibly keep this place, it's falling down around your ears. I'm willing to up my offer by ten thousand dollars.'

Roslin said in a voice like a steel blade, 'How clever of you to wait until the first rainfall to do so.'

'Elementary, I would have said.'

She gave him a brilliant smile. 'The first snowfall should merit at least twenty thousand, wouldn't you say?'

The edge in his tone clashed with hers. 'You'll be long gone by the time the snow falls, Roslin.'

'Don't count on it, Tyson.'

'Don't be a fool! Your great-aunt was a tough-minded old biddy who liked birds better than people and didn't care who knew it. But you're young and beautiful and you'd die of loneliness up here by yourself. You *can't* stay here!'

The truth in his words struck home, infuriating her. She said sweetly, 'And once you're married you won't be able to drop in like this, will you?'

'This is not a social call,' he rapped.

He had given her the perfect opening to tell him about Liza's visit, which had not been a social call either. But somehow Roslin could not bring herself to do it. She said evenly, 'Fine. I am refusing your very generous offer. So you can leave now.' She stood back to allow him free access to the door.

He stayed where he was. 'Dammit, I've never known anyone who could get under my skin the way you can!'

She scowled at him. 'The feeling's entirely mutual.'

'Show me what's wrong with the damned fireplace.'

'Stop swearing!'

'Better I swear than release my feelings some of the other ways I can think of,' he snapped.

Under the soot she blushed. Then she fluttered her lashes at him. 'That's certainly a hellish, awful, damned dreadful dilemma,' she said.

There was no mistaking the laughter this time. 'A dilemma whose horns I feel we should avoid. The fireplace, Roslin.'

The hearth was a soggy, smouldering mass of ashes and charred wood. Tyson peered up the chimney. 'Birds' nests,' he said succinctly.

'How appropriate,' Roslin murmured.

'Have you got a long-handled broom?'

'There's one in the back porch.' She ran to get it.

When she came back, Tyson was examining the photos on the mantel. 'Your parents?'

Wondering if he would recognise her mother, hoping he would not, she nodded. 'Let me look after the chimney, you're too well-dressed.'

'And deprive me of the role of Sir Galahad?' He took the broom from her, regarding her clinically. 'You're more beautiful than your mother. But you have the same chin.'

'Determined.'

'Pig-headed.'

'Resolute.'

'Obstinate.' Briefly he rested his hand on her shoulder. 'They're dead, aren't they?'

She seemed to shrink a little. 'Six years ago,' she muttered. 'A jet crash in France.' At which point Colby, her father's brother, had taken over her life and her potential career. Colby was not at all like her darling, vague, lovable father. As she had learned to her cost.

'I'm sorry,' Tyson said, investing the conventional words with genuine sympathy.

'Are either of your parents alive, Tyson?'

His face closed. 'No.' Leaning the broom against the fireplace, he hauled his sweater over his head and passed it to her. 'Here goes,' he said.

Five minutes later a tangle of twigs, fortunately unoccupied, had tumbled into the hearth, and Tyson was as sooty as Roslin. 'Hold still,' she ordered, reaching up and extracting a tuft of grey down feathers from his hair. 'Epitaph for Great-Aunt Mellicent,' she said solemnly.

Quite suddenly he began to laugh, a hooting bellylaugh that was irresistibly contagious. Roslin joined in, laughing until her ribs hurt and the tears were trickling down her face and she was rid of all the trials of the past twenty-four hours. Then, just as suddenly, she stopped. Tyson took her in his arms and started kissing her.

She was familiar by now with his fierce energy, just under the surface, only just under control; and with his almost angry demand for response. Before she could be overwhelmed, she struggled against his hold, wrenching her head free and muttering, 'Wait, Tyson...please.'

His eyes were like storm clouds. Before he could say anything she went on, speaking from some deep well of intuition, 'I know you can be masterful and demanding and macho. Show me another side of yourself.'

He frowned. 'What are you talking about?'

'Kiss me like this.' Venturing into the unknown, Roslin slid her palms up his chest and kissed him with exquisite tenderness on the lips, moving her mouth very gently. Then she stepped back.

He had stood there like a stick. 'So I was too rough— I'm sorry.'

She sought for words, she who could not have been more inexperienced in the realm of kissing. 'You always seem so angry. So tough. Isn't there a place for tenderness? For cherishing? Rather than control and domination?'

Tyson said flatly, 'I don't know.'

Unexpectedly, tears filled her eyes. 'Try,' she said.

He hesitated. Then he bent his head and found her mouth, all his movements tentative, unsure of themselves. But when he kissed her, they were not driven kisses, full of inward torment; they were much more gentle, lingering to explore and enjoy, savouring the sweetness of her response; and in them Roslin entered a new land where she had never been before, a land drenched in sunlight that she claimed as her own in gratitude and wonderment. His hands were stroking her body through her shirt, pressing her against his hips so that she could feel his arousal. Her heart began to beat in slow, heavy strokes.

He moved back from her a little, his hand smoothing the shining weight of her hair. His hunger was naked in his face, his grey eyes reflecting something of her own wonder. 'Sea-witch,' he whispered. 'See what you do to me?'

'I...I seem to be caught in my own spell.'

He tried to joke, although his voice was husky. 'What did you call it, an awful, damned dreadful dilemma?'

'Hellish was mentioned too, I believe.'

The words were nonsensical, but the soft-spoken comments had allowed each of them the time to recover, to draw back from the brink of something for which possibly neither of them was ready. Tyson glanced over his shoulder at the fireplace, and said more strongly, 'If you bring me a garbage bag, I'll clean up the mess.'

Roslin did as he asked. Then, when he had gone upstairs to wash his hands and face, she put dry paper and wood in the hearth, and risked putting a match to it. This time the smoke obeyed the laws of physics. She sat on the rug in front of the fireplace, hugging her knees. Her body felt lethargic, while the wonder of Tyson's kisses still lingered in her face. The flames crackled higher.

When Tyson came back she was gazing into the fire, a small figure in jeans and a dirty shirt with a sheaf of black hair down her back. For a few long seconds he watched her in silence. Then he said harshly, 'You've cleaned the whole house.'

Her head swung round; his tone had wiped the smile from her face. She said lightly, 'Right down to washing the floors in the middle of the night.'

He was not amused. 'You're settling in.'

His hands were shoved in the pockets of his canvas trousers and his features were set in grim lines; Roslin could have wept for the loss of the man who had kissed her so sweetly only a few minutes ago. 'I suppose I am,' she said matter-of-factly.

'I worry about you here,' he said violently. 'It's far too isolated. At the price I'm offering you, you could buy a house anywhere in the state—anywhere in the country—a sensible house with neighbours and a roof that keeps out the rain. You could afford forty acres full of flowers if that's what turns you on, and a fleet of gardeners to go with it. Be reasonable, Roslin, for goodness' sake!'

'You make me feel anything but reasonable,' she replied, hugging her knees more tightly. 'If you're going to badger me, Tyson, go home.'

Over the chatter of the fire she heard his sigh of exasperation. He was prowling the room like a caged tiger, restless, full of the pent-up energy that was so characteristic of him, and again she marvelled that he should have come back to the prim and proper village of Carmel. Perhaps originally he had returned for only a short visit, she thought unhappily, but meeting Liza had changed his plans.

He had stopped in front of the radio that rested on the ugly but enduringly solid mahogany desk. He turned the knob. A pianist was playing the opening bars of Beethoven's Opus 57 Sonata, the F-minor arpeggios descending and ascending so simply yet so evocatively, followed by the four bass notes that Roslin could have played in her sleep... She had performed that sonata in Budapest; she never wanted to hear it again. Leaping to her feet, she said frantically, 'Turn it off, Tyson!'

He frowned. 'That's the *Appassionata*, isn't it? It's one of my favourites.'

'Tyson, please turn it off!' She covered her ears with her hands, her face distraught. 'I can't bear to listen to it.'

He snapped the radio off, the music ending in midbar. Slowly Roslin lowered her hands. Although the competition in Budapest had ended a month ago, the wounds it had dealt were as raw as if it had been yesterday.

'What's wrong, Roslin?'

Her cheeks were drained of colour and her eyes looked black as soot. For a moment she wondered if she could tell him the whole story, for the first time pour out all her conflict and pain to someone who, she was almost sure, would understand. Colby had never understood. Colby had been furious with her performance, and even more furious with the rebellion it had fostered.

Yet what did she really know of Tyson? Perhaps he was more like Carmel, and Liza, than she thought. Perhaps he would use her story as yet another lever to remove her from this house. Perhaps he would think, like Colby, that she should have tried harder and forced herself to the top despite the cost. That she was a quitter.

She said in a thin voice, 'That particular piece of music reminds me of something I would much rather forget—that's all.'

'Something pretty powerful.'

She rubbed her forehead with a hand that was still not quite steady. 'I just want to forget it!'

He said forcefully, 'I don't know how you can feel that way about music...it's the only thing that's ever been able to make any sense out of life for me...the only thing to give it meaning.'

A desert lay behind those words, a sweep of scorched and arid sand where love and affection had perished for lack of sustenance. Her throat aching, Roslin whispered, 'I used to feel that way too.'

He did not ask what had made her change. Instead he said, 'How old are you, Roslin?'

Taken by surprise, she muttered, 'Twenty.'

'I thought you were older... Are you going to university?'

She shook her head. Since her parents had died she had not even gone to a regular school. Colby had hired tutors for her, to give her more time to practise.

'So what do you do?' Tyson continued relentlessly.

'I suppose you could say I'm unemployed,' she said wearily. 'Sooner or later I'll have to do something about that—but not right now.'

'Certainly if you're going to keep this house, you'll have to.'

'Tyson,' she said tightly, 'apart from an uncle in Boston, I don't have another living relative in North America. I only met my great-aunt once, I know, but at least she was a blood relation. I'm determined to live here. I need this house. I will not allow you or anyone else to drive me out of it. To control me.' Her knees were trembling. 'You'd better go,' she finished in a low voice.

He picked up his sweater. 'Don't think I've given up, though, will you?' he said levelly. 'I'll see myself out.'

When the front door closed, Roslin put her head on her knees and began to cry. When she stopped, the flames had died down and the ashes were grey in the hearth.

The next afternoon the telephone rang. Wishing it would be Tyson, yet simultaneously dreading the sound of his voice, Roslin picked up the receiver. 'Hello,' she said.

'William Smith here, Roslin,' said a jaunty voice. 'How are you today?'

Her eyes were puffy and her bones ached. 'Fine,' she said.

'I'm combining business with pleasure, if I may. Business first. Mr Waldron called me earlier, he's hoping you're ready to accept his most generous offer for your property.'

'No, William, I'm not.'

'Now, Roslin, I would strongly advise you——'

She could have told him of Tyson's higher offer. But she was frightened of Bradleigh Waldron, and did not want Tyson incurring his enmity. 'I'm not looking for advice,' Roslin said.

'You cannot possibly stay in that house in the winter!'

'I'll worry about that in December, William. What was the pleasure part of your call?'

'I wanted to ask you out for dinner tomorrow night,' he said, not sounding nearly as jaunty as he had at the beginning of the conversation.

William was in line for a commission if Bradleigh purchased the property, she decided shrewdly; perhaps even if Tyson bought it. Poor William. She also decided she was not yet lonely enough to accept his invitation; music, she was sure, would not give meaning to William's life.

'I'm very busy at the moment,' she said smoothly. 'Perhaps another time.'

The short silence was definitely huffy. 'Mr Waldron won't be very pleased to hear that you're refusing his offer,' William snapped.

'Give him my sympathy,' she said tartly. Modifying her tone with an effort, she added, 'Thank you for phoning, William. Goodbye.'

She put down the receiver, cursing the day Great-Aunt Mellicent had put her affairs in the hands of Cuthbertson and Smith, and looked around abstractedly. The telephone was in the hall, whose oak floor shone and whose wallpaper had been dust-mopped. The whole house was clean, except for the piano room. She could mow the grass. Or tidy the shed.

Feeling oddly restless, she went outside. The sun was hot but the wind had come up, buffeting the trees and chasing the clouds across the sky. It would be a nice afternoon to find a sheltered spot by the shore and curl up with a book, she thought. She would take a picnic supper.

She packed some sandwiches and went down the shore, and after she had eaten fell asleep there, lulled by the waves. So it was nearly dusk when Roslin returned to the house. The sun was setting, the trees black against an orange sky, the house throwing long, distorted shadows on the grass. For the first time she saw the small-paned windows as secretive; the house seemed hunched in its hollow of land, brooding over its memories. Over its dead, she thought with a chill in her spine.

As her footsteps crunched on the gravel, she wished she had left a light on inside to welcome her home and give the illusion of habitation. She unlocked the front door and stepped inside, her ears acclimatising themselves to the creaks and groans of an old house in the wind. Carefully she locked the door behind her.

After cleaning up the few dishes in the sink, Roslin went upstairs and had a bath, and would strenuously have denied that the wail of the wind and the amount of bubble-bath she used were in any way related. She discarded her old burgundy housecoat for a caftan she had bought in Florence, a very dramatic garment that was stiff with embroidery and gold thread. She looped her hair high on her head, and accented her eyes with mascara.

Dutch courage, my girl, she told herself, knowing she disliked the keening of the wind quite intensely. She would paint her fingernails, which she could grow longer now that she was not playing the piano. She might even paint her toenails.

In the living-room she put two coats on both sets of nails and rubbed cream into her hands; but although darkness now enclosed the house it was still too early to go to bed. Not having to practise the piano gave her a lot of spare time, Roslin was beginning to realise. For a moment she regretted throwing away the key to the room upstairs; she could have played to herself, for pleasure. But then she hardened her heart. She had run away from the piano and all that it represented.

She had started a book by Dorothy Dunnett that afternoon. Fetching it from the kitchen, where she had left it in the picnic basket, Roslin settled down in one of the chintz armchairs to read. The book soon absorbed her attention, and the noises of the old house fell into her subconscious. She read on, curled up in the circle of lamplight.

She was not sure what it was that distracted her. She raised her head from the book, all her senses alert. Then she heard it: a scratching sound against the shingles, too regular and too loud to be caused by the wind. She closed the book, straining her ears. The sound stopped.

She had not drawn the curtains; she rarely did, for who was there to see her? Now she found herself wishing she had pulled the old flowered drapes over the pitch-black panes of glass. She would feel safer...

The scraping started again, from the other side of the
fireplace this time. Every nerve tense, her fingers
clutching the book, Roslin listened, her mind scurrying
for a rational explanation. A deer. A tree branch. A
raccoon looking for food. Or, more likely, a group of
boys from the village out for mischief.

She felt a measure of relief. That was it. The house
had been empty for several months after her great-aunt
had died, and any vacant property was always vulnerable.

The scratching stopped. Silence. In it, Roslin heard
the pounding of her heart and the wail of the wind, and
knew she was frightened.

Someone knocked on the front door.

CHAPTER SIX

IT TOOK every ounce of Roslin's courage to get up from the chair and walk to the front door. But, before she opened it, she looked through the antique glass to see who was there. The front step was empty.

Torn between anger and terror, she went back to the living-room and marched over to the window above the desk to draw the curtains. A face appeared, pressed against the glass panes.

Roslin screamed. The face disappeared.

Wringing her hands, she wondered crazily if she had imagined it. For the face had not been a normal face; the features had been hideously stretched and distorted. A gargoyle. A creature of nightmares. And no boy could reach those windows, they were too far off the ground.

The tapping resumed by the fireplace. In the narrow window that was inset parallel to the chimney the face appeared again, grimacing at her. It wore a mask, she thought dimly, wondering if she was going to faint. A stocking mask like gunmen wore. The eyes looked like sockets in a skull.

Again, the face vanished. Its absence was worse than its presence, for at least when it was peering through the glass she knew where it was. What it was doing. Roslin ran for the telephone in the hall. Her hands were shaking so badly, she could hardly turn the pages of the directory. Buckton . . . Carmel . MacDonald . . . Marston . . . McCully, Tyson.

She dialled his number with trembling fingers, pressing the receiver to her ear, her palms slippery with sweat. The phone began to ring.

Into her brain dropped the horrible suspicion that the man outside might be Tyson. Three rings. Four. Tyson was not at home because he was outside her house.

Tyson had gone through the house. He had warned her about the inadequate locks and the lack of security and the isolation. Tyson wanted to buy the house. He had told her only yesterday that he would not give up.

Please, no. Don't let it be Tyson.

The front door knob slowly turned, one way and then the other. Roslin moaned with a terror beyond anything she had ever known in Budapest, and through the receiver heard Tyson's voice say, 'Hello.'

'*Tyson?* Thank heaven...' The masked face wavered through the antique glass and she gave a sharp, indrawn cry.

'Roslin? What's wrong?'

Then she felt the wind stir the hem of her caftan and through the open dining-room door saw that one of the windows was open. The curtain was flapping lazily back and forth. 'Tyson!' she gasped. 'Oh, please...' Dropping the receiver so that it banged against the wall, she ran for the living-room and picked up the poker. Her back to the fireplace, her nerves screaming with tension, she waited for the masked figure to appear.

Nothing happened. Each creek of the joists and each rattle of the windowpanes made her pulse leap, but no one stole down the hall or burst through the living-room door. The minutes ticked by, as long as hours, and still she waited. Her fingers ached where they were curled around the poker. Her wrist muscles trembled, just as they had after a particularly long session with Ferrolino in Florence, during the series of lessons when she had met Aloysha... Then she forgot about Aloysha as she heard, unmistakable over the howl of the wind, the roar of an engine, the screech of brakes, the sound of footsteps running towards the house. Tyson.

He banged on the door.

Moving very slowly, she crept into the hall, the poker held like a sabre in front of her. Through the door Tyson yelled, 'Let me in, Roslin! Or I'll break the damned door down.'

She would have known his voice anywhere. She hurried to the door, fumbled with the key, and released the lock just as Tyson threw his weight against the oak panels. The door burst open, flinging her to the wall. The poker flew from her hand. Tyson grabbed her by the shoulders and said hoarsely, 'Roslin, are you all right? Are you hurt? For pity's sake, answer me!'

She wanted to say that he was swearing again, but she could not find her voice. Falling into his arms, she buried her face in his chest and held on to him as tightly as she could.

He kicked the door shut behind him and put his arms hard around her, rocking her back and forth. 'It's all right, there's nothing to be afraid of. I'm here, I'll look after you, you don't have to be frightened...'

His heart was pounding as hard as hers, and when he had burst through the door he had been white-faced. 'There was a man,' she muttered. 'Looking through the window.' She shuddered. 'He had a mask on.'

'*Here?* Just now?'

She nodded against his shirtfront. 'He-he was turning the doorknob when you answered the phone... I was so afraid that you weren't going to answer!'

'I was in the shower... I almost didn't hear it.'

For the first time she looked up. 'Your hair's wet.'

His smile was wry; he was still white about the lips. 'I thought you were being murdered, Roslin—I wasn't going to fool around drying my hair. You're damn lucky I've got clothes on.'

He was wearing rugby shorts, a T-shirt and running shoes on bare feet. 'That's the T-shirt I borrowed in the van,' she quavered. Her eyes huge in her face, she added, 'Tyson, thank you for coming to my rescue.'

'You're welcome.'

'I didn't know who else to phone.'

'Prowlers. Birds' nests. All part of my Sir Galahad role. Have you got a flashlight?'

'In the kitchen. Why?'

'I want to check for footprints.'

'She clutched his sleeve. 'Don't leave me alone!'

'It's OK, Roslin, I'm sure the guy left as soon as he saw you phoning,' Tyson replied, patting her hand. But although he had been gentle, his eyes were turbulent with anger. 'You're damn lucky he didn't cut the wires.'

She said weakly, 'You're back to swearing again.'

'Little wonder! I'm biting my tongue not to say I told you so. I warned you about the isolation. I warned you about Bradleigh. But you were determined to stay here, weren't you?'

Like a match touched to dry grass, antagonism flared between them. Tyson was already in a towering rage, she rather belatedly realised, while her own fears were easily translated into anger. 'So am I supposed to let a two-bit land developer drive me off my own property?' she blazed. 'What would you do in my shoes, Tyson? Meekly pack your bags and leave?'

'I'm a man, it's not the same.'

She stamped her foot. 'What kind of an answer's that?'

'If a guy in a mask breaks into my house, I could knock him to the ground. What would you do, Roslin?'

'I'd hit him with the poker,' she snapped.

His eyes sparked with something other than rage. He said lazily, 'You look quite magnificent in that outfit...like the princess in *Aida*. What was her name...Amneris? Were you expecting company?'

Roslin had forgotten about the caftan. She said shortly, 'I don't like wind.'

'So you painted your fingernails.'

She glowered at him. 'Stop laughing at me!'

He said evenly, 'If I don't laugh at you, I'll be hauling you off to bed.'

'Oh.' Colour tinged her pale cheeks. 'You mustn't do that,' she said.

'Exactly. Show me the flashlight, Roslin.'

Knowing she had lost that round, Roslin led the way to the kitchen, the caftan swishing round her ankles. Her gaze flickered nervously to the uncurtained windows before she knelt down to search in the cupboard under the sink. She produced the flashlight and passed it to Tyson. 'If you're going outside, I'm coming with you,' she announced.

'Oh, never leave me,' he warbled, off-key.

'I am not a poor maiden!'

He was testing the batteries. 'No, you're not. You're a stubborn, opinionated, pig-headed young woman whom I can't get out of my mind night or day—particularly night—and who's turned all my plans upside-down. I knew where I was going until you came along. Or I thought I did.'

Roslin discovered she liked what he was saying very much. She gave him what she hoped was a good imitation of Carmen's seductive smile and said, 'I'm not like Liza.'

'No, you're not like Liza. And no, I am not going to kiss you—I know my limits. Put your boots on, Roslin, and we'll play Sherlock Holmes.'

Her boots were on the mat by the back door. Roslin pulled them on, hitched up her skirts, and said blandly, 'Lead on, Watson.'

He gave a choke of laughter, flexing his muscles. 'Now I know what you want me for . . . and it's not my brains.'

The T-shirt fitted him much better than it had fitted her, and the ripple of tanned flesh did peculiar things to her peace of mind. 'You're just another pretty face,' she said agreeably, unlocking the back door.

She led the way around the house, and in the wind-torn darkness their mission no longer seemed cause for laughter. When she came to the flowerbeds by the living-room windows she said tonelessly, 'He must have stood somewhere around here.'

Tyson shone the flashlight on the garden. The phlox and bee balm had been trampled, and several large footprints were sunk in the mud. 'He was at the other window, too,' Roslin said in a small voice.

They traced the footprints all round the front of the house, and saw where the man had forced the latch on the dining-room window. Tyson said thoughtfully, 'I didn't pass anyone on the road. He probably hid in the woods. Let's go inside.'

The first thing Roslin did was draw all the curtains. Then she put the kettle on and made a pot of very strong tea. She had a shrewd idea of what was to come; nor did she have long to wait. As soon as they were seated in the living-room with the tea and crackers and cheese, Tyson said, 'You can stay at my place tonight... I'm not leaving you here alone.'

Needing time to think, Roslin remarked, 'I don't even know where you live.'

'When I came here six months ago I bought the house next to Liza's. She had moved back with her family after the divorce.'

Smothering all kinds of unruly responses, Roslin said, 'Then you don't need me staying overnight. Obviously.'

He said impatiently, 'Liza would understand.'

'I wouldn't, in her shoes. Anyway, if I leave the house, the man might come back and vandalise it.'

'Does that really matter? Even you must see you can't live here now, Roslin.'

She said, remembering Budapest and searching for the right words, 'Once before in my life I was really frightened. To the point where I couldn't function and I let a lot of people down, including myself. Myself most of all. I'm not going to do that again, Tyson... so I need two favours of you. One, that you'll stay here until daylight. Two, that you'll lend me the van tomorrow so I can go to the nearest pound and buy two of the biggest, meanest dogs they've got.' She looked him full in the eye. 'Will you do that for me?'

There was a long silence. Then Tyson said, 'You're really desperate for a home, aren't you?'

He had said home, not house. Her eyes filled with tears. 'Fairly desperate, yes,' she gulped.

'And you've got guts, I'll give you that. What frightened you so badly before, Roslin?'

Again she was tempted to tell him. But she knew if she did it would bind him to her more closely than he already was; and she was not so inexperienced that she did not recognise how badly she could be hurt by Tyson. She said carefully, 'I've been told you belong to Liza. If that weren't true, then possibly I would tell you. As it is, I'm afraid of sharing too much with you ... after all, what's the point?'

He said with sudden savagery, 'I don't even belong to myself any more.'

But he had not denied that Liza had a claim on him. Sick at heart, Roslin said, 'Will you do me those favours, Tyson?'

'Yes.' His breath hissed between his teeth. 'And if you get hurt in this débâcle, I'll never stop blaming myself for not booting you back to Boston.'

She was far more likely to be hurt by him than by any of Bradleigh's manoeuvres. But Roslin kept this thought to herself. 'Thank you,' she said. 'I'll make up the bed in the spare room; excuse me a minute.'

The spare room smelled pleasantly of lavender and lemon polish, and knowing Tyson was downstairs made her earlier fears seem exaggerated. He was checking all the doors and windows when she went back down. 'The bed's made,' she said. 'Do you want me to show you which room you're in?'

He followed her up the stairs. She showed him the spare room and said awkwardly, 'I hope you'll sleep well.' He looked wide awake, his formidable energy in no way diminished by the lateness of the hour, so that

she was aware of how foolish her conventional words
sounded even as she said them. 'Goodnight,' she muttered, and fled across the hall.

After closing the door of her room, she got into bed
immediately. She had two other plans for tomorrow that
she had not shared with Tyson; she would need an early
start. Closing her eyes, she eventually fell asleep.

When she went downstairs in the morning Tyson
already had the coffee brewed. They ate breakfast
making rather constrained conversation, then Roslin
rummaged in the shed for the leashes and collars she
had seen there before, from the days when Great-Aunt
Mellicent must have kept dogs; without being asked,
Tyson began repairing the two old kennels under the
trees at the back of the house. This gave Roslin the
chance to make her phone call.

Robert Petrie, the head trustee of her parents' money
in Boston, would be happy to speak to her, said his secretary. After they had chatted about his vacation, Roslin
plunged into her request, trying to be factual rather than
emotional, stressing the market value of her inheritance
rather than her own need for a home away from Colby.
She must have done a good job. Hedging his acceptance
with various precautionary phrases, Mr Petrie seemed
to think a loan for the repair of the roof would not be
a problem.

Greatly encouraged, Roslin went out to help Tyson.
Handing him some nails, she said, 'Where's the nearest
dog pound, Tyson?'

'Buckton. I'll go with you.'

'I can manage on my own.'

'If you're going to get two dogs, you'll need help.'

'Then could I have an hour's shopping before we get
the dogs?' she asked, wishing she did not have to be
devious but almost certain he would disapprove of her
plan.

'Sure. Pass me that piece of two-by-four, would you?'
So when they got to Buckton they separated, agreeing

to meet in the delicatessen for lunch at noon. A couple of enquiries led Roslin to her destination, and after a five-minute wait she was ushered into Bradleigh Waldron's office. He was sitting behind an oak desk that was more like a fortress than a desk, and he did not get up when she entered. Blowing a cloud of cigar smoke in her direction, he said, 'Come to accept my offer, Miss Hebb?'

'What makes you think I'd do that, Mr Waldron?'

He tapped ash into a crystal ashtray. 'Thought you might have reconsidered.'

He had not offered her a seat. Roslin looked straight at him and said, 'Nothing's happened to cause me to reconsider.'

His eyes narrowed in their folds of fat. 'Then why are you here, Miss Hebb?'

'I spoke to my trustee this morning. He's fully prepared to authorise money to repair the house so that I can live in it this winter. Which I am planning to do.' Robert Petrie had actually requested that she send photographs and estimates before he would authorise anything, but she did not feel she had to tell Bradleigh every detail.

Viciously he crushed the end of the cigar in the ashtray, grinding it into the glass. 'You can't live in that place alone!'

'Try me,' Roslin said, although the small, telling gesture made her skin crawl.

Almost visibly, he changed tactics. He said smoothly, 'Now, why would a pretty little thing like you want to live in Carmel? You planning to catch yourself a man? Tyson McCully, for instance?'

If the prowler had hung around last night, then Bradleigh would know that Tyson was the one who had come to her rescue. 'Of course not,' she said haughtily.

'He's worth a lot of money, is Tyson. Enough for Liza Westhaver to turn a blind eye on his background.

His parents—— '

'Tyson's parents don't——'

He overrode her ruthlessly. 'His daddy was the town drunk. Had a nasty temper, they say. Lots of times Tyson came to school with more bruises than he could have got fighting in the schoolyard. They say old man McCully used to knock his wife around, too. Likely justified, mind you—she was no better than she should be. Not what you'd call a maternal woman.' Bradleigh extracted another cigar from a sterling silver box on the desk. 'Kind of surprised me when Tyson showed up here six months ago—figured once he'd shaken the dust of Carmel off his boots he'd never come back.' The flame from a silver lighter flared briefly. 'I wouldn't want you thinking Tyson might relieve you of your property. Because I can outbid Tyson, Miss Hebb. Can and will.'

She should not have come here, Roslin thought sickly. She had involved Tyson; and Bradleigh was still convinced he would get the place. Trying to close her mind to the image of a little boy with grey eyes and a bruised face, she said with a hauteur that Colby would have recognised, 'Neither of you will get it. Goodbye, Mr Waldron.'

'You can find me here when you change your mind,' was his parting shot.

She could think of no brilliant repartee with which to respond. Gritting her teeth, she stalked out of the office and down the stairs. When she reached the bottom step, a man pushed open the glass door that led to the street. Tyson.

She said furiously, 'What are you doing here?'

'I thought you were shopping, Roslin,' he said ironically, eyeing her arms, which were empty of packages.

'I found out this morning I can get the money to repair the house. I thought if I told Bradleigh, it would get him off my back.'

'But you've now decided you were overly optimistic.'

She blurted, 'How did you get that scar over your eye, Tyson?'

'What's that got to do with Bradleigh?'

Nothing. Everything. 'It shows up because you're so tanned,' she said evasively.

'I fell down the stairs when I was a kid.'

She was quite sure he was lying, and equally sure she was not about to challenge him. If Tyson was ever to tell her about his parents, it would have to be of his own free will. 'Why are *you* going to see Bradleigh?' she asked pointedly.

He gave her his wolfish grin and drawled, 'I thought I might mention to him that if there were any repeats of last night's performance I personally would break every bone in his body.'

She looked at him in silence. 'You're interfering in my business, Tyson.'

'You're the one who phoned me last night. *In extremis*, as it were.'

She could scarcely contradict him. 'Do you think he'll listen to you any more than he listened to me?'

'I do believe he might.' The grin was downright demonic. 'Bradleigh and I go back a long way.'

'Just like you and Liza,' she flashed.

The grin disappeared. 'I'll meet you at the delicatessen at noon,' Tyson said and took the stairs two at a time.

Roslin walked back to the main street, and in record time bought new batteries for the flashlight and enough groceries, including dog food, to last a week. She entered the delicatessen at five past twelve. Tyson was sitting down reading a newspaper. She said dispassionately, '*You* seem to be in one piece—how's Bradleigh?'

'Only Bradleigh's ashtray is no longer in one piece. The desk proved beyond me.'

'Tyson! What did you do?'

'Too many people are afraid of Bradleigh; very bad for him.'

'What did you do?'

He lowered the newspaper. 'I had to get his attention first. Hence the ashtray. Then I managed to get the point across that he shouldn't lay as much as a finger on you if he values living. That's all.'

Regrettably, Roslin was, at some rather primitive level, quite pleased with Tyson. She snorted. 'He-man stuff.'

'Directive counselling.'

A smile tugged at her lips. Picking up the menu, she said with considerable satisfaction, 'Do you realise what we've accomplished today? I can stay in the house. The roof will be fixed and Bradleigh won't bother me again. Maybe I don't need the dogs.'

'You're getting the dogs. And you're forgetting something. I said *I* wanted the property, Roslin.'

In a flash of pure jealousy she said, 'You'll never live in my house with Liza.'

'Perhaps I should live there with you.'

She looked up, coloured, paled and sputtered, 'Don't be ridiculous! What would you do that for?'

'To get you out of my goddamned system.' He smiled charmingly at the waitress who had appeared at his side. 'Number four and a Budweiser, please.'

'Number six, please,' Roslin said faintly. 'With a glass of milk. Tyson, you're swearing again.'

'Maybe if I got you out of my system, I'd stop.'

'Out of your system—as if I'm a dose of salts! Why don't you try a ten-mile run instead? Or a trip to the Arctic?'

'Living with you would be more fun.'

In complete exasperation Roslin said, 'Do you know what my biggest problem is? I never know when you're serious and when you're joking. But I do wish you wouldn't joke about things that are serious.'

'I think you've been too serious for too long,' he said with considerable perspicacity. 'Six years too long?'

The waitress brought his Budweiser. Roslin picked up the other section of the paper and rustled the pages busily. 'This is a crazy conversation. Drink your beer.'

'How long do you think it would take me to get you out of my system, Roslin?'

She had grabbed the sports section. Trying to focus on the batting averages of the Boston Red Sox, she said rapidly, 'I refuse to speculate on a subject which is both frivolous and mendacious. What does RBI mean?'

'You see, you need me to interpret the important things of life. Runs batted in. I think it could take quite a while, Roslin.'

'And then what?' she said nastily, abandoning the maze of incomprehensible figures as her bagel appeared. 'Would you ask me to move out so you could move Liza in?'

'I rather doubt that I would do that.'

For a moment the heap of bean sprouts blurred in front of her eyes. With sudden intensity she said, 'Tyson, are you in love with Liza?'

He put down his glass. With matching intensity he replied, 'When I was thirteen I was madly in love with Liza. She was blonde and beautiful and utterly unattainable, the princess of the tower for whom I would have slain a whole herd of dragons.' His smile was so wry that it hurt Roslin somewhere deep inside. 'Unfortunately there weren't any dragons in Carmel, and Liza would have turned up her aristocratic nose at the corpses if there had been. Not long after that I left Carmel, and didn't come back until six months ago. Whereupon I found Liza not only available but interested . . .' Moodily he picked at his salad, and finished with a bitterness that horrified Roslin, 'So I started going out with her. The princess of the tower, you see, had become the woman next door.'

He had not answered her question. Or had he? Roslin said very gently, 'Do you mean you left home when you were only thirteen?'

'I'd turned fourteen by then.'

Instinctively she covered his hand with her own. 'That's too young—I know, because I was only fourteen when my parents died.'

'So was I.' He gave her a smile in which the savagery was only thinly masked. 'Things we have in common. Reasons we should live together. You're right, this is a crazy conversation, and how did it get started, anyway?'

She jerked her hand back as if he had struck her, and gazed at her bagel, wondering how she was going to choke it down. This was not the time to realise how easily she could fall in love with Tyson. To realise that what she most wanted to do was put her arms around him and give him the love she was becoming increasingly certain he had never had.

Falling in love will take away your freedom, she thought frantically. Freedom is what you want most. Not Tyson.

In total silence they ate their lunch and left the restaurant. The animal shelter was as heart-wrenching as Roslin had anticipated, and she had a hard time leaving with only two dogs, the one a shaggy and joyful mongrel to whom she related instantly, the other a morose bloodhound whose sad eyes had followed her around the room. Neither looked mean. But they were undeniably large.

Tyson drove her home, accompanied her and the dogs on a tour of the property so they could get to know their boundaries, and helped her feed them. Then he said abruptly, 'I'd better go home. Roslin, you'll call me if there's even a suspicion of anything out of the ordinary, won't you?'

'Nothing will happen,' she said confidently. The sun was shining and dusk was far away.

He gave her arm a little shake. 'You'll call me,' he rasped.

'OK—I promise.'

'I hate like hell leaving you here,' he said violently, climbed in the van and drove off without looking back.

The dogs watched his departure, the bloodhound looking as depressed as Roslin felt.

She said out loud, 'I don't understand that man!' As the mongrel licked her hand, she added gloomily, 'I don't understand myself, either.' The bloodhound sighed.

CHAPTER SEVEN

ROSLIN was preparing supper when the dogs began to bark. The mongrel's bark was high-pitched and full of its own cleverness, the bloodhound's a lugubrious baying. Roslin hurried to open the front door.

Liza was standing beside her sleek little car. The dogs, whom Roslin had temporarily named Mutt and Jeff, were sitting twenty feet from Liza, between her and the house. Greatly encouraged, Roslin called them off. 'Hello, Liza,' she said cordially. 'Will you come in?'

'Where did you get those?' Liza said with barely concealed distaste.

'The pound.'

'The pound in Buckton.' Liza pounced. 'How did you get there, Roslin? You don't have a car.'

'Tyson took me.'

The pale blue eyes flared with as much emotion as Liza was capable of. 'Tyson spent the night here, didn't he?'

Roslin sighed. 'Why don't you come in and I'll make a cup of tea, Liza? It isn't the way you think.'

'I want you to stay away from Tyson! He's changed since you arrived.'

'For the better?' Roslin asked naughtily.

'I don't know what's wrong with him,' Liza said irritably. 'But it's something to do with you. So leave him alone.'

'He stayed last night because Bradleigh Waldron hired someone to come out here and prowl around the house to scare me off. He took me to the pound to get the dogs so that he wouldn't have to stay again. He slept in the spare room.' The pale blue eyes now showed no emotion whatsoever. 'Liza,' Roslin said with more truth than

96

diplomacy, 'Tyson isn't the right man for you. You must know that.'

'I want him,' Liza said inflexibly.

Roslin had not expected to feel sorry for Liza. She said gently, 'Didn't your divorce teach you that we don't always get what we want?'

A telltale spasm crossed Liza's face. But then she said coldly, 'I want to get married again. Tyson will be a suitable partner.'

'You used not to think that way. Years ago.'

Liza glared at her. 'He's a different person now.'

Roslin's temper was rising, too. 'You mean he's got more money.'

Liza put her hands in the pockets of her beautifully cut walking shorts. 'That's right,' she said.

Roslin sighed. How could she argue with someone so armoured against the real issues? The real emotions? 'I don't think anyone's ever loved Tyson for himself,' she said carefully. 'Amy and Annabel are probably the ones who come closest.'

'Two old maids,' Liza sniffed.

'Yes. Two old maids,' Roslin agreed drily. She looked down as Mutt, the mongrel, collapsed on her foot with a silly grin. 'I'm going to take these two for a walk. You can come if you'd like...it seems silly for us to argue about Tyson, who's a man with a mind of his own if ever there was one. Why don't you come?'

'I invited Tyson for dinner tonight—so I have to get home,' Liza said with a glittering smile. 'Some other time, perhaps. In the meantime, I really would appreciate it if you'd stay away from him.' She got in her car and gunned it down the driveway.

Roslin watched the dust settle. She had made a tentative offer of friendship and it had been refused. And Tyson, a man with a mind of his own, was having dinner with Liza.

'I'll have to learn some new swear-words,' she announced to the dogs. 'Damnation does not seem adequate. Let's go for a walk.'

The walk, a very energetic one, helped somewhat. Roslin ate supper with her nose buried in the book by Dorothy Dunnett, cleaned up, wrote a couple of letters, and then brought the dogs in and went around the house drawing all the curtains. She had made up her mind that she was going nowhere tonight: she had to prove to herself that she could stay in the house alone. She read until ten-thirty, not sure whether she was more bothered by the tiny noises of the old house settling for the night or by the thought of Tyson at Liza's. Then she went to bed.

Mutt leaped up on the quilt, snuffled around with his tail wagging, then curled up in a ball and went to sleep. Jeff circled the room, tested the rug suspiciously, and collapsed on it with a thud and one of his world-weary sighs. He put his nose on his paws and gazed sadly at Roslin.

'I know the feeling,' she said. 'Go to sleep, Jeff,' and eventually followed her own advice.

She awoke to daylight and a distinct pride in herself for having slept so soundly. Mutt licked her ear. Jeff yawned. She leaped out of bed, feeling unquestionably light-hearted. Tyson had not stayed at Liza's overnight, she would bet Great-Aunt Mellicent's inheritance on that. Tyson did not want to make love to Liza, he wanted to make love to her, Roslin; and in that area he would not compromise himself. Or so she thought. Singing to herself, she pulled back the curtains and looked out at the inlet, where the mist hovered over the still, grey water and a heron was flapping ponderously between the trees.

My place, Roslin thought. The place where I'm free of the past, free of music and of Colby. My own place.

She would visit Amy and Annabel today. She liked them for themselves; but they also represented community and the need for neighbours, and she was guilty of neglecting them.

Mid-morning she tied up the dogs, not yet trusting them to stay home without her, and cycled the mile or so to the two identical cottages on the outskirts of the village. As she knocked on the door of the first one, Annabel poked her head out of the door of the second. 'We're over here today,' she said. 'Do come in, dear; I said to Amy only yesterday we hadn't seen you for a while.'

The cottage was exactly as Roslin had expected it to be: immaculately clean, daintily decorated, crammed with antiques and old pictures. First Annabel took her on a tour of the garden, pointing out every plant that Mellicent had ever given her; then she and Amy fluttered around inside, pouring tea from a silver service, insisting Roslin eat far too many cakes and cookies, and showing her all their photographs of her great-aunt. Roslin was thoroughly enjoying herself. But she also wanted to talk about Tyson, and her hope that his name would come up naturally was diminishing.

Finally she said without finesse, 'I saw Tyson yesterday.'

Amy looked at Annabel, her eyes brightening. 'Did you, dear? Such a nice man.'

Briefly Roslin described the trip to the pound without going into the reason behind it. Annabel remarked, 'So he's looking after you, how nice.'

'I expect he worries about you in that big place.'

'All alone.'

'Of course, Mellicent was alone too.'

'But Mellicent was different.'

'I hope he'll feel better soon.'

'He did look dreadful, didn't he?'

Roslin's head had been swinging back and forth to follow this dialogue. 'What do you mean—what's wrong with him?' she squawked.

'We saw him in the drugstore early this morning.'

'Buying aspirin.'

'The flu, dear.'

Roslin said in distress, 'He should have phoned me—
I would have bought them for him.'

'Maybe you should visit him,' Amy said craftily.

'Just to make sure he's all right.'

Said Roslin gloomily, 'Liza's probably there with her
hand on his forehead. Being cool and competent.'

'Liza went to Boston for the day.'

'Shopping.'

'Oh,' said Roslin.

'We'll wrap up some little cakes for you to take.'

'And we'll give you a bottle of our blackcurrant wine.'

'My father used to say it would cure a horse of the
heaves and a man of everything but the gout,' Amy finished triumphantly.

Roslin laughed. Then she said bluntly, 'Bradleigh
Waldron told me about Tyson's parents.'

'Oh, dear,' Amy murmured.

'We used to invite Tyson here sometimes. For meals.
But he was a proud boy, and wouldn't often accept,'
Annabel mused.

'He didn't get enough to eat.'

'His father drank every penny his mother made.'

'They say she used to—well, you know, dear—for
money.'

'I wouldn't blame her,' Annabel said vigorously.
'Better than starving.'

'I suppose so,' Amy said doubtfully.

'Of course it was. Don't be provincial, dear,' Annabel
chided.

Roslin had heard enough. She was beginning to
understand why Tyson had come back to Carmel and
bought the house next to Liza's. Understand but not
condone, she thought unhappily. 'I should go,' she said.
'I think I will drop in to see him. Where is his house?'

The directions seemed straightforward and a few
minutes later Roslin left, loaded with cake and black-

currant wine. It was drizzling with rain as she pedalled along with her poncho flapping in the breeze, the tall trees keeping her relatively dry. Before she reached the main street she turned to the right, heading for the water. The first house was an arrogant stone mansion with the name Westhaver emblazoned on its carved gateposts, the grounds occupying at least twenty acres; Roslin pulled a face and turned into the next driveway. Tyson's van was parked behind the house.

This house also was stone, a cold, grey stone; the shrubs and trees were artistically placed, but there was not a flower in sight. Roslin disliked the place instantly.

She walked up the back steps and rapped on the door. No one came. She knocked again, louder this time. From inside a male voice yelled something indistinguishable. She waited, clutching the cakes and wine.

Tyson looked through the glass. His face grew still when he saw her. He unlocked the door and held it partly open, his only garment a pair of jeans; he was unshaven, his hair tousled, his eyes dark-circled. He said, 'Roslin.' Then he ran his fingers through his hair and gave his head a little shake. 'I've got the flu—you'd better not come in.'

'I know you have the flu, Amy and Annabel told me. That's why I came.'

'You might catch it.'

She favoured him with her most dazzling smile. 'If I do, you can come and visit me.'

He scowled at her. 'There's no point in you visiting me now—there's nothing you can do.'

He moved to close the door in her face. But Roslin had been prepared for this, and quickly stuck her foot in the gap. 'If we're going to argue about this, you'd better let me in—at least temporarily,' she said, 'because otherwise you'll add pneumonia to the flu. Anyway, I've brought you something from Amy and Annabel, and I wouldn't dare tell them you wouldn't let me in; they think you're such a nice man.' She fluttered her lashes. 'You wouldn't want to disillusion Amy and Annabel, would you?'

'You should be selling encyclopaedias, you've got the right personality,' Tyson said unpleasantly.

She edged past him into the back porch. 'Pushy, you mean.'

'That wasn't the word I had in mind, but it'll do.'

'Shut the door, Tyson, even though it's the only thing that's keeping you upright. And then go back to bed. I'll be up in a minute to see if I can get you anything.'

He closed the door and leaned against the wall. His face was paper-white, the skin stretched across the bones. 'We'll have the argument first and then you can leave.'

'I'm perilously close to bopping you on the head with Annabel's blackcurrant wine,' Roslin said. 'Which is not the use for which it was intended. I'm not here to rape you! I'm here to help.'

'I don't need help.'

'So I ask you to come to my rescue, but you can't handle the reverse ... oh, Tyson, please go back to bed, you look as though you're going to drop.'

'I keep telling you, I can manage on my own!'

Suddenly her eyes widened. What if Amy and Annabel were wrong? What if Liza had cancelled her trip? She said in a hollow voice, her eyes huge, 'Liza's upstairs.'

'Liza went to Boston this morning for three or four days!'

'Did she know you had the flu?'

'She knew I wasn't feeling well.'

'Some friend she is.'

'She knows I don't want anyone fussing around.'

Roslin did not like his choice of words. 'You know what your problem is? You can't admit you're human like the rest of us. That you might have to ask someone for help. To surrender control.'

'Don't be silly.'

'Have you ever in your life allowed a woman to look after you?'

'No.'

'Then today is lesson number one. Upstairs, Tyson.'

He pushed himself away from the wall and said roughly, 'I could wring your neck. If I had the energy.'

Interpreting this admission of weakness as a tacit acceptance of her presence, Roslin put the cakes and wine on a nearby shelf and hauled the poncho over her head, emerging with her hair in wisps about her face. Then she pulled off her boots. She was wearing well-fitting white canvas trousers with a low-necked, flame-coloured silk shirt and barbaric gold bangles at her ears and wrists: an outfit she had thought would interest Amy and Annabel.

Tyson said in a strangled voice, 'Stay out of my bedroom in that rig—I'm not dying, for heaven's sake.'

For the first time Roslin felt on the defensive. 'I didn't know I was coming to visit you,' she said. 'I didn't choose my clothes with you in mind.'

'Sure,' he sneered.

In one small word he had succeeded in cheapening her gesture of friendliness; she was not doing very well in that department. Her shoulders sagging, she said, 'I suppose I have been pushy, although I didn't intend it that way. I'm sorry, Tyson... I'll make sure you get upstairs safely, then I'll get out of your hair.'

She turned away, pretending to unwrap the wine, afraid that she was going to cry. In his view she had been brash and insensitive, forcing herself on him when he didn't want her help. He didn't want her here at all. And it would be her fault if he caught pneumonia.

A hand fell heavily on her shoulder. She ducked her head, the black sheaf of hair baring her nape. 'I've said I'll go,' she muttered. 'You win—I won't bother you again.'

'I—don't go, Roslin,' he said hoarsely. 'I didn't mean to hurt you—it's my turn to say I'm sorry.'

She was shredding the brown paper bag between her fingers. He reached around and took her hands in his, so close that she could feel his body heat against her back. 'Please stay,' he said. 'I'm sorry if I was rude to you.'

'You interpret everything the worst possible way! I only wanted to help.'

'I agree. I'm a rotten, mean-mouthed jerk who doesn't deserve you, and if I don't get back to bed soon I'm going to fall flat on my face at your feet.'

She twisted in his arms, her midnight-blue eyes filled with alarm. 'You do look awful,' she exclaimed.

Clamping his hands on her shoulders, swaying a little, he said, 'I feel awful.'

Suddenly discovering that she did not want him to have to beg for help, Roslin said as casually as she could, 'Put your arm around me—can't have you falling flat on the floor, you'd be there for the duration.'

With a smile full of self-derision, Tyson did as she asked. Their progress across the hall and up the stairs was slow and shambling, for Tyson was weaker than she had thought, his skin burning to the touch. He had a double bed in a room which otherwise could have passed for a monastic cell; the sheets were tangled and damp with sweat, so she made him sit on the nearest chair while she changed the linen.

When she had finished, he pushed himself up and went round to the far side of the bed. 'Vamoose,' he ordered. 'I haven't got anything on under my jeans.'

Her situation suddenly struck her: she was in Tyson's bedroom and they were alone in his house. A tide of painful colour crept up her neck into her cheeks.

Tyson was grasping the headboard for support, his face full of strain. 'This is going to sound like an exceedingly stupid question and I don't really know why I'm asking it...but why are you here, Roslin?'

She said with complete honesty, 'When Amy and Annabel told me you were sick, I knew I had to come. I didn't stop to think. I just came.'

Sweat had sprung out on his forehead. He said harshly, 'What does all this mean? You and I . . . what the hell's happening?'

'I—don't know.'

He ran his fingers through his hair and said impatiently, 'Turn your back.'

She obeyed, hearing the scratch of his zipper, the tiny sound as he tossed his jeans to the floor, the creak of the bedsprings. 'Can I get you anything to eat?' she asked, staring out through the bedroom door.

'Ginger ale with lots of ice in it. Nothing to eat, thanks.'

The rest of the house was as spartan as the bedroom, the furnishings expensive and in good taste, but unrelieved by the touches of colour, the plants and works of art that give a dwelling its character. The whole place looked temporary, thought Roslin, as though Tyson had bought it on a whim and then had not bothered with it since. The van seemed more like his home than this expensive stone house. She poured ginger ale into a tumbler, added ice-cubes, and carried the glass upstairs.

Tyson was already asleep, breathing erratically, his face burrowed in the crook of his elbow. She put the glass on the bedside-table and left the room. After making a sandwich in the kitchen she went into the living-room to eat it, and there, taking up the entire end wall, she discovered the personality of the house.

Tyson's stereo equipment was both expensive and knowledgeably chosen, and his collection of records, tapes and compact discs rivalled her father's. Tyson was a dark horse, she thought. A lot of the recordings were no longer available; he must have haunted secondhand shops to acquire them. With a sharp pang of loss, she wished her father could have met him.

She put on an old Heifetz recording very softly, and ate her sandwich; it was a long time since she had listened to any music. Then she tiptoed upstairs.

Tyson was tossing and turning, his face and shoulders
damp with sweat. Even as she watched, he heaved himself
half-way across the bed, muttering, 'No—no!' under his
breath, and then subsided into the pillows again.
Frightened, not sure if he was delirious or having a
nightmare, Roslin touched her palm to his forehead.

His eyes flew open. Seizing her wrist with crushing
strength, he pulled her sharply downwards so that she
fell across his body, bruising her breast against his
ribcage. She cried out with the sudden pain, trying to
brace her hands on the mattress.

His eyes cleared. With an appalled, 'Roslin!' he released her wrist.

It had been an instinctive move of defence, a swift
and effective reflex that betrayed more about Tyson's
rough-and-tumble life than any amount of speech could
have. Roslin lay still, feeling the heavy pounding of his
heart through her shirt, watching the muscles move in
his throat as he swallowed. Then she made her body relax
and put her arm over his shoulder. 'You must have been
dreaming,' she said gently.

'Yeah...' His forehead was resting on the soft flesh
of her inner arm, where the veins were blue under the
skin. 'You feel so cool,' he murmured.

'What do you dream about, Tyson?'

'Oh, stuff from the past,' he said evasively. 'Do we
ever get rid of it?'

So she was not to be told. Her one desire to bring him
comfort, she began stroking the hair back from his
forehead with her free hand, her fingers sensitive yet
strong; with a tiny sigh of surrender he closed his eyes,
turning his face into her elbow. His breathing deepened.
Within seconds he was asleep in her arms as trustingly
as a child.

His face was only inches from hers, his chest rising
and falling under her palm. This was the second time
she had lain with him; how much better she knew him
now than on the night they had slept together in the van.

Experimentally she ran the words through her mind. I love you, Tyson...I love you?

So was this love, this strange mixture of comfort, trust and desire? As a child she had been comforted by her parents and had trusted them implicitly, so that those facets of love were known to her; but this blind urge to unite her body with that of the man in her arms was as new to her as Tyson was new. For Roslin was achingly aware of the body so close to her own, and knew if Tyson had not been ill she would not have dared to have lain with him in such intimacy. But was it love? One side of love?

She had no one to ask. And like a dash of cold water in her face she realised how flimsy was the trust between her and Tyson. She had not trusted him with the whole sorry story of Colby, and he had not trusted her with his dream, or with his past. Perhaps freedom was struggling out of the bonds of the past, she thought humbly. Recognising those bonds, so that they no longer controlled you.

With a sigh of defeat Roslin closed her eyes, drifting in and out of sleep because Tyson was so restless. But eventually the fever broke and he quietened, and she herself fell into a deeper sleep.

She woke to find him lazily caressing her cheek; she was still lying fully clothed on top of the covers. He drawled, 'Did Florence Nightingale provide this kind of care?'

Any remnants of sleep fled her brain. 'It's a new concept,' she replied. 'Its intent is to defeat the macho male ego.'

The grey eyes were sparked with humour and desire. 'More than my ego is involved here, honeybunch.'

'You're feeling better,' she said severely.

'Very weak. Luckily for you.' He yawned. 'Also starving. And not a thing in the refrigerator to eat.'

Roslin glanced at her watch and sat up in a hurry. 'It's nearly seven o'clock,' she squeaked. 'The dogs need feeding. Tyson, I could drive you to my house and make dinner for you... will you let me do that?'

She was sitting on the bed, her shirt creased, her hair falling over one shoulder. Her expression was full of hesitancy, almost as though she already regretted her proposal. Tyson said with a strange urgency, 'Roslin, are you afraid of me?'

She had not expected his question. 'I could be hurt by you very easily... so I'm afraid of that. And I hate it when you shut me out.' For a moment her eyes met his. 'Almost as though *you're* afraid of *me.*'

'Perhaps I am,' he said soberly. 'You force me to let my guard down. To show my weaknesses. It's been a long time since I've let anyone see my vulnerabilities— not since I was a kid.'

She said passionately, 'But I'd never use them against you!'

'No... I don't believe you would,' he said in the same strange voice. 'You're the most honest person I've ever met—and I say that even though I know there are secrets you're keeping from me. Parts of yourself you won't share.'

'I'm not ready yet,' she said. 'Anyway, the same is true of you.'

'Yeah... Maybe we should back off, Roslin. Go our separate ways. Because the more we share, the harder that will be.'

From the depths of her heart she cried out, *'No!'*

'I don't want you to be hurt,' he said savagely.

She twisted to face him, her body like a flame in the brilliant shirt. 'Are you going to marry Liza?'

He said, choosing his words with care, 'I've never spoken of marriage to Liza, I wouldn't want you to think that. She, for her own reasons—hurt pride from her divorce, I should imagine—would like to marry me... she sure wants me to get hold of your property, I know that. But Liza suits me, Roslin. She doesn't make any demands on me. Emotional demands. She goes her way and I go mine.'

'And is that all you want out of life?' Roslin demanded.

Steadily he kept her gaze locked with his. 'I'll be honest with you. When I first came here and found that Liza was available, I toyed with the idea of marriage. The kid from the wrong side of the tracks marrying the rich man's daughter, the classic American dream...I told you that when I was thirteen Liza was a symbol of all that I couldn't have. But the conclusion I'm coming to is that I'm not the marrying kind, Roslin, not even to someone like Liza who would ask very little of me. I've been a loner for too long.' He gave her a crooked smile. 'You saw the fight I put up before I'd even let you in the door...I haven't allowed myself to need anyone for more years than you've been around. All of which is a very long answer to a very simple question.'

She did not want to hear the warning implicit in his words, a warning that applied to her as much as to Liza. She said with a touch of desperation, 'I didn't come to Carmel to get involved with anyone, either—I came to be free! Accountable to no one. Complete within myself. Now I don't even know the meaning of the word, not since I met you.'

Tyson said with an attempt at lightness, 'You can call off your dinner invitation, I won't get mad.'

But his jawline was tense under the pallor of illness, and Roslin knew her answer related to far more than the cooking of a meal. If she changed her mind about dinner, she might not see Tyson again. She was dangerous to him; and he did not want her to get hurt. Producing a smile that almost worked, she said, 'Scared I can't cook? You're not getting out of it that easily, Tyson McCully.'

'A man's gotta do what a man's gotta do,' he intoned. Then his own smile faded. 'Don't forget what I said, though, will you, Roslin?'

'I will not plan an August wedding,' she said with a toss of her head.

'You can't afford to, not if you're going to have the roof fixed,' he said wryly.

But Roslin was following her own train of thought. 'I don't understand, if you've never proposed to Liza, why you were so keen to buy my house,' she said.

He was pleating the sheet, his head bent. 'When I was a kid, I used to do odd jobs for your great-aunt. I always loved her property. . . as near to paradise as one could get. Or so I thought at the age of ten. I suppose it came to symbolise something to me over the years—if I could buy out Mellicent Cowper, I'd arrived.' He shifted his shoulders. 'Goes to show how wrong you can be.'

Another piece of the jigsaw had fallen into place. 'So it had to do with Carmel,' said Roslin. 'Not Liza.'

Tyson nodded. Then he pushed the sheet back. 'You'd better get out of here, I'm going to get dressed. Which could take a while. My strength is not the strength of ten.'

She said primly, 'I won't offer to help.'

'If you do, I'll accept, and dinner could be long delayed,' he replied with a gleam in his eye that made her tremble.

She climbed off the bed and headed for the door. When she was a foot away from it she said, 'Talk is cheap, Tyson,' and fled down the stairs.

He had warned her off. But she was almost sure he was not going to marry Liza.

CHAPTER EIGHT

TYSON'S strength was not even the strength of one, let alone ten, and as soon as they arrived at Roslin's he went to bed. Roslin prepared a light supper of pasta, salad and fruit, took it upstairs and ate with him in the spare room. He fell asleep again after supper, so she took the dogs for a walk along the shoreline. When she got home it was dusk, but the house looked welcoming rather than secretive, and the knowledge that it contained Tyson made her lips curve in an involuntary smile; she had no intention of waking him up to go home.

After spending nearly an hour grooming Mutt in the back porch, a process he seemed to enjoy, she had a bath and went to bed herself, putting on a very pretty nightgown of Portuguese cotton whose modesty did not sacrifice femininity. She was two-thirds of the way through the Dorothy Dunnett book. She settled down to read until she felt sleepy.

At twenty to one she was glued to the last chapter when she heard Tyson get up and go to the bathroom. Then his steps padded across the hall floor. 'Roslin?'

Jeff growled and Mutt wagged his newly combed tail. 'Come in,' said Roslin, and put the book face down on the bedspread. 'How are you feeling?'

'You didn't have to let me sleep half the night.'

She should be used to Tyson in jeans and nothing else; she was not. 'No, I didn't,' she said equably, trying to ignore the unmistakable hostility in his tone. 'I thought you needed the rest. You look better.'

'I feel better,' he answered curtly. 'So I'll get dressed and go home.'

She sat up a little straighter. 'Afraid you'll turn into a pumpkin?'

111

'I've got to get out of here . . . I don't have to spell out my reasons, do I, Roslin? You're not that stupid.'

She thought of Liza, who never made any demands on him, and said, 'Why don't you spell them out, Tyson? Just to make sure we both understand.'

'Better than that, I'll show you.'

He strode into the room and sat on the bed. Mutt thumped his tail on the bedspread while Jeff eyed him reproachfully from the floor. Roslin said sharply, hating the anger in his face, 'Don't, Tyson!'

'Don't what? Don't do this?' Very deliberately he took her breasts in his hands, caressing her flesh through the thin fabric of her nightgown, tracing the hard peaks of her nipples. Through her tangled emotions the piercing pleasure was like a clarion call; it shivered across her face as her eyes darkened to the blackness of night. Then Tyson began kissing her, lowering his weight on her, his fingers now laced in the silky hair that covered the pillow.

His kisses were deep. Willingly Roslin parted her lips to them, forgetting his anger, forgetting his motives, only aware of the dart of his tongue and the flooding tumult of her own desire. She gripped his bare shoulders, loving the taut, smooth planes of his back, the softness of the hair that curled on his nape, never wanting the kisses to end. And far at the back of her mind a tiny voice whispered that this was why she had not woken him; this was what she had hoped would happen.

He was fumbling with the pearl buttons at the neckline of the nightgown, buttons that went to her waist. Then he pushed the folds of cotton back. His hand, firm, warm, sure of itself, captured the swell of one breast. She gave an involuntary cry of delight, and kissed him with all the passion of her nature.

The next few minutes were never very clear in her mind. Dimly she heard Mutt jump to the floor as Tyson ripped the covers down. Then she felt his fingers dance on her thigh. As he clasped her to him, her breasts crushed against his chest, she ached to be naked for him, no barriers between them, only this surging hunger for completion that was beyond anything she had ever experienced.

The denim of his jeans rubbed against her knee. She reached for his waistband, knowing in her heart that to join with Tyson in this act of love would be the fullest expression of her freedom. Had it not been inevitable from the moment they had met?

His jeans had a metal clasp. As she struggled with it his body suddenly grew still, the utter, threatening stillness of the centre of the storm. Then, so violently that she cried out with shock, he wrenched himself free of her, rolling over to lie on his stomach, his head buried in his arms.

The sobbing, indrawn breaths were her own, the tattoo in her ears that of her heartbeat. Roslin seized his shoulder. 'Tyson—what's wrong?'

He shook his head; the light fell on the thick, dark hair and on the ridged muscles along his spine: the body that in a primitive way she had laid claim to that night. It was hers, she thought fiercely. Hers alone. Never Liza's.

Very slowly he pushed himself up. His face was haggard, his eyes full of pain. He rasped, 'When I woke up here, in your house, and saw the light from your bedroom, I wanted to make love to you so badly that it hurt. That was why I had to get out of here—I don't have to tell you that.'

For the first time he looked at her. She was so close that the pain in his features was mirrored in her eyes; because she had not thought to cover herself, the bedside-lamp cast shadows on her breasts and hollowed throat. His face convulsed. He said harshly, 'We can't make love, Roslin!'

It took all her courage not to pull the gown tight to her body. 'Why not?' she whispered. 'How could something that felt so right be wrong?'

He was staring at the bed. 'You're ten years younger than me; from what you've told me I would gather you're a virgin; and I would also gather you're not protected against a pregnancy. Those are three good reasons.'

Roslin had not inherited her mother's chin for nothing. 'But they aren't the real reasons, are they, Tyson?'

He shook his head. 'No. They're not the real reasons.'

'Tell me the real reasons.'

Once again Tyson looked up. He said flatly, 'I'm afraid of falling in love with you.'

His eyes were trained on her face. She drew the neckline of her gown together and said, 'Would that be so awful?'

'I've told you I'm a loner. That I've never allowed myself to need anyone. I can't change that, Roslin.'

'Can't or won't?'

'Can't!' he exploded. 'I was eight years old when I vowed I'd never get married, and I've lived that way ever since. Free of commitments. Knowing that this whole romantic fallacy called falling in love is just that— a fallacy.'

Roslin said with a careful lack of emphasis, 'Am I the first person who's caused you to think of changing your mind?'

'I suppose you are.' He hesitated. 'You're a beautiful woman, Roslin, beautiful in so many ways. For all your youth, you're generous and passionate and fired with intelligence. How do you think I'd feel if I strung you along with lovemaking and fake promises, just to get you in my bed? I can't do it. I won't do it. Because I can't risk hurting you.'

'Maybe it's too late,' she said in a low voice.

'No, it's not too late. Which is why I'm getting out of here now, and I'm not coming back.'

'What do you mean?' she gasped, feeling a knot of fear tighten in her breast.

'I mean we shouldn't see each other again.'

Her face was blank with shock. 'Ever?'

'Ever. It's best that way.' Tyson got up from the bed, his movements those of a much older man, and said, 'Sell this place, Roslin. Or give it to the bird society if you can't stand the thought of dealing with Bradleigh. And then go back to Boston where you belong.'

'Don't you want to buy it any more?' she flashed.

'Having known you, I don't think I could live here. Not alone. And certainly not with Liza.' He gave a humourless laugh. 'How's that for honesty?'

Horribly afraid of the answer, yet knowing she had to ask, Roslin said, 'So what will you do?'

'I don't imagine I'll hang around in Carmel much longer. I shouldn't have come back at all.'

'You mean we'll just disappear from each other's lives? Tyson, we can't do that!'

'We can and we will. And in a few weeks you'll understand it was for the best.'

He could have been quoting Colby. 'Stop telling me what I'll feel!' she cried. 'You're running away, Tyson. Running away from involvement and intimacy because you're afraid of them. *You* might think it's for the best to leave Carmel—*I* don't have to agree.'

'That's another thing,' he interjected with a matching anger. 'I know damn well there's been some kind of major crisis in your life recently, and that *you're* running away from something. Or someone. I don't know why you're determined to live like a hermit in an old house that's falling down around your ears—but I do know you'd better sort that out before you start imagining you're in love with me.'

He had a genius for finding the weak spots in her armour, she thought, and said furiously, 'So my attempts at seduction are just an avoidance mechanism, is that it?'

'That's it.'

He had tarnished something beautiful. Roslin's temper died and she said in a choked voice, wishing she could do up every one of the pearl buttons, 'I hate this conversation.'

'I don't care for it much myself,' Tyson responded levelly. He levered himself up from the bed. 'I'm going to get out of here. No long speeches, no touching farewells. But take care of yourself, won't you?'

He was walking round the end of the bed. Her tongue seemed to be stuck to the roof of her mouth. With preternatural clarity she watched Mutt sniff at the cuff of Tyson's jeans and noticed how Jeff was still wearing his expression of mournful reproach; the image was imprinted on her brain as if someone had clicked the knob of a camera.

Tyson left the room. She could hear him moving around in the spare room, then he went downstairs; the fourth step and the seventh creaked as they always did. The front door opened and closed. The engine of the van roared into life, the gravel crunched under the tyres, and the sound of the motor faded to silence.

He had gone. She was alone. Roslin stared blankly at the opposite wall, wondering why she felt so cold, wondering if she would ever be warm again.

Two weeks passed. Roslin slept a lot, for that passed the time. She also worked ferociously in the garden and walked for miles with the dogs. However, she went into Carmel as little as possible, terrified of meeting Tyson and having to make artificial conversation with him in the queue at the grocer's. He had not left town; she knew that much from Amy and Annabel.

She had told the two old ladies that she and Tyson were no longer friends: a necessary euphemism for a situation whose complexity she could not bear to describe. They had shown true delicacy by asking no questions and true concern by inviting her for tea as often as she cared to come. She was very glad they were her friends.

Roslin's other pursuit was to think a great deal about freedom. Because Tyson was leaving her strictly alone and Colby had still made no attempt to get in touch with her, she was accountable to no one, her time her own, to be used as she saw fit. She had the freedom that she had craved.

She genuinely tried to adopt Tyson's point of view that she was too young and too confused to fall in love. That her feelings for him were a consequence of being uprooted from the house where she had lived since she was a child, and of losing the outlet of music. Nature abhorred a vacuum. Nature had filled the vacuum in her life with Tyson. A neat and tidy theory that, try as she might, did not make her miss him the less and could not diminish her feelings.

She tried calling them puppy love. Hero worship. Even pity. She tried rooting them out as vigorously and as finally as she rooted out the weeds in the garden. She tried telling herself that the last thing she needed was another man in her life controlling her.

None of these strategies made the slightest difference. Roslin missed Tyson deeply and continually, as if a part of herself was missing. Her inherited property was big enough for her to exhaust herself physically and thereby cope with the newly awakened hungers of her body. But Tyson had also awoken her to the joys of male companionship and shared laughter, to the need to give of herself to another. And Amy and Annabel, no matter how sweet they were, could not help her there.

It was Tyson she wanted. It was Tyson she could not have.

She spent one whole day endeavouring to convince herself she should go back to Boston, for what good would Carmel be to her once Tyson was gone? But a force stronger than reason seemed to be telling her to stay. Her father had called such forces gut instincts and had placed great faith in them. Roslin, following suit, called two contractors to come and give her estimates

for the repairs on the house, and took photographs to
send to Robert Petrie.

The contractors came on a Friday. On Saturday
evening, about ten o'clock, Roslin was sitting in the
living-room knitting and watching television when Mutt
suddenly leaped up from the carpet and raced into the
dining-room, barking raucously, his nails scrabbling on
the hardwood floor. Jeff, more sedately, loped to the
front door and let out an ear-splitting howl. Roslin
dropped a stitch.

She put down her knitting, picked up the poker, and
went out into the hall. Mutt was doing his best to climb
through the closed window in the dining-room, still
barking hysterically, while Jeff looked amazingly wide
awake as he padded up and down in the hall, pausing
every few seconds to bay at the ceiling. She was immensely glad of their company.

Not stopping to think, for if she had she could not
have done it, Roslin marched into the dining-room and
dragged back the curtain. To her everlasting relief there
was no masked face pressed to the glass. But in the circle
of light from the front door she would have sworn she
saw a dark figure slip between the bushes at the side of
the house.

Bradleigh had disregarded her own warnings and
Tyson's. Bradleigh was trying once more to frighten her
out of her property.

Roslin went to the telephone. She could not call Tyson,
but she could call the police. When she did so, a calm
male voice assured her a patrol car would be there within
five minutes. While she waited, marching up and down
the hallway, Mutt abandoned the dining-room for the
back door. Jeff also disappeared into the kitchen, his
howls sounding like a soul in torment.

The wail of a siren added to the racket. Distorted by
the antique glass, the red and blue lights on the patrol

car swirled against the faded wallpaper in the hall. Roslin unlocked the door.

'Down, Mutt! Down, Jeff!' she yelled, grabbing the dogs by their collars and wishing she had taken the time to come up with more original names.

'Trouble with a prowler, miss?' asked the policeman.

He was large and solid in his blue uniform. She tried very hard not to think about Tyson, and explained what she had seen and that she had had trouble before. The other policeman, smaller, younger, and obviously captivated by her smile, joined him from the car. They circled the house, crashing through the bushes.

When they came back, the older one said laconically, 'Footprints by the back door.'

'You live here alone?' asked the younger; while he admired her smile, he plainly did not think much of her common sense.

She tilted her chin. 'Yes.'

'Be smarter if you moved into town. Pretty isolated here.'

Roslin refrained from telling him he was not the first person to give her this advice. Then the older man said, 'We'll file a report, miss, and we'll make a point of keeping an eye on the place. Not much else we can do. You OK to stay here tonight, or you want us to take you into town?'

'I'll stay,' she said steadily. 'Thanks for coming so promptly.'

She locked the door behind them and went to bed, and for the first time since Tyson had left she cried herself to sleep. But her tears accomplished something. When she woke in the morning she had made a decision. It stayed with her as she fed the dogs and had breakfast and answered a phone call from Annabel, who wanted to know why she had called the police the night before. When she had answered Annabel's questions without, she hoped, unduly alarming her, Roslin went upstairs to the room with the locked door. She had to live without

Tyson, that was clear. She could not live without her music as well.

The knob rattled, but the lock held firm. Roslin fetched a knife from the kitchen, and then her credit card, but neither worked as they did in the movies and the door remained locked. Putting on some heavy clothes, she went outside, rounding the house until she came to the patch of brambles where she had flung the key.

An hour and many scratches later she found it. Clutching it victoriously, she headed for the house, where she put some cream on her face and hands and went upstairs. The lock yielded to the key.

The room smelled faintly of the climbing roses that nodded below the window. The piano was dusty. Roslin lifted the lid and touched middle C, and the note reverberated in the silence. Rolling up her sleeves, she sat on the bench and began very slowly to play scales.

Three hours later, totally absorbed, deaf to anything else, she was playing Chopin from memory, for there was no music in the bench. Some of the nocturnes and waltzes were as familiar to her as her own name; or so she had thought. But Roslin, in the weeks since she had left Boston, had experienced loneliness, passion and terror, jealousy and pain; and as her fingers curved over the keys she knew the music had changed, that it was charged with a new maturity, an emotional strength that had been lacking in Budapest. She had assumed she would be able to escape from Tyson through her music. But the music could not be an escape from Tyson. The music had become Tyson.

She played that most rugged of nocturnes, the Opus 48 No. 1, losing herself in the crashing chords, deaf to everything else in the world. Then she drifted to her favourite, the E minor, with its soft, repetitive bass and clear treble notes, each one perfectly chosen, speaking to her directly of the loss of Tyson, of the aching void she had tried so hard to fill.

Music had betrayed her. She broke off in the middle of the nocturne, resting her forehead on the piano's cold wood and closing her eyes in utter despair.

From the doorway a voice said quietly, 'Roslin, you play beautifully.'

For a moment Roslin thought she had imagined the voice, that it was part of her deep longing for the man who had removed himself from her life because she demanded too much of him. She raised her head, her face blank. Tyson was standing at the door.

He was wearing canvas trousers and a blue shirt; his face was open to her, unguarded and bemused, and she remembered how he had once told her that music was the only thing that could make sense of his life. How long had he been listening? Had he heard in the simple notes her own longing and her pain, revealed to what she had thought was an empty room? She said, tamping down an eruption of anger that frightened her with its force, 'What are you doing here?'

'Amy told me you had to call the police last night—what happened?'

Roslin said succinctly, 'A prowler at the back door.'

His face tightened. 'Wait until I see Bradleigh.'

'I don't want you to go near Bradleigh...what happens here is nothing to do with you any more. Which is why I phoned the police, and not you.'

'You should have called me! I was so damned angry after I talked to Amy that I got in the van and came roaring up here to tell you off. And discovered what you've been hiding from me.'

'You have no right to come here—and certainly no right to tell me off, as you so charmingly put it,' Roslin said with icy calm. 'The concert's over, Tyson. Go home.'

'Why did you lock this room?'

'Tyson, I'm not in the mood for an inquisition. Particularly from you. You're the last person I would have phoned yesterday evening... now get out of here!'

He walked further into the room. 'I've been listening long enough to know you're immensely talented. You can't lock that kind of talent away, Roslin.'

The legs of the bench rasped on the floor as Roslin stood up. 'Stop trying to control me!'

'I hit a nerve there, didn't I? So who's been controlling you? This uncle you never talk about?'

'Tyson,' she fumed, 'two weeks ago you walked out of here in the middle of the night, determined to protect, among other things, your virtue and your narrow little life. You now seem to be under the impression you can wander back any time you please. Well, you're wrong. You made a decision—you stick with it.'

'Maybe I made the wrong decision.'

The quieter his voice became, the angrier she got. Advancing on him, she hissed, 'You should have thought of that at the time. I want you to leave—now!'

'Make me,' he said lazily.

'Mutt!' she yelled. 'Jeff!'

'They're outside. Guarding the front door, which you left unlocked... Why is your face scratched, Roslin? Did you have a fight with the prowler under a rose-bush?'

'When I moved in, I threw the key to this room into a patch of brambles,' she snapped. 'Today I went looking for it.'

He gave a bark of laughter. 'How melodramatic.'

'How delightful that I amuse you,' Roslin retorted. 'Leave, Tyson—or I'll be calling the police again.'

He was standing between her and the door. 'Feel free,' he said amiably.

Free. How could she feel free when Tyson was within a hundred miles of her? Roslin sauntered up to him, holding his eyes with her own, and when she was within a foot of him, ducked, pivoted, and whirled around him. Or that was her plan. But somehow he was in the way, so that she cannoned into him instead, with such force that the breath was knocked from her lungs. His arms went around her. He said with overdone solicitude, 'Careful, Roslin...didn't you learn in physics that two bodies can't occupy the same space at the same time?'

Through gritted teeth she said, 'I must have missed that lesson. Let go!'

'I don't remember learning that two bodies can't co-exist side by side, though.'

She said with mingled fury and indiscretion, 'When the two bodies are ours, there's a danger of spontaneous combustion.'

'So you haven't forgotten that.'

His body heat, the clean, masculine scent of his skin, the pounding of his heart...she had forgotten none of them. Staring at the weave of his shirt, Roslin said desperately, 'Tyson, you're not playing fair. Two weeks ago you left here forever. Today you walk back in as though you own the place...you can't do that, it's too hard on me.'

There could have been no mistaking her sincerity. He held her away from him. 'Will you answer one question? Why did you look for the key today?'

She said with complete truth, 'Because I figured if I was going to have to do without you, I couldn't do without music as well.'

His body was very still. 'You missed me.'

'Yes, I missed you!'

'Why?'

If she had not known him well, she might have dismissed the question as facetious or unimportant. She said helplessly, 'I don't know if I can explain it... I like you, even though we fight such a lot. I want to know more about you. I—I'm attracted to you.'

'You mean you want to go to bed with me?'

She nodded, not looking at him. 'And I feel sometimes I could tell you anything and you'd understand.'

'Try me—tell me about the piano.'

Roslin was still standing loosely in the circle of his arms. Gazing at him, her face troubled, she said, 'And then what, Tyson? If I tell you about the last six years, I'm sharing a huge part of my life with you. Are you then going to pull your disappearing act? Pardon me, that's too much intimacy, I've got to go now?'

'So I'm a coward,' he said grimly.

She did not deny it. 'We either have a relationship or we don't. But we can't be on one week and off the next.'

'And neither of us can make it a shallow relationship.'

She repeated with gentle irony, 'I'm not like Liza. Neither, I'm convinced, are you.'

'It's all or nothing, then.'

The words terrified her. 'All the things you said about me are true. I'm young and inexperienced, and I'm afraid of being hurt. Maybe you were right last time—maybe we should opt for nothing.'

'I don't know about you, but for me it was one hell of a long two weeks.'

From Tyson, this was practically a declaration of love. It gave Roslin the courage to say, 'I wish I were more experienced. So I'd know if the way I feel is sort of routine—ho hum, here we go again—or unique. Rare. Special.' Briefly she rubbed her cheek against his shirt-front. 'Do lots of people feel the way we do?'

Tyson said drily, 'I'm less young than you and more experienced, and I think it's rarer than you might suppose.'

'Experienced!' she spat. 'I hate all those other women.'

She felt the laughter deep in his chest. 'There weren't that many of them, Roslin. I didn't have the time or the inclination to be Don Juan.'

'Do you know something? I don't even know what you do for your living.'

'I saved every penny I made in the mines, then I started investing in the stock market.' He shrugged. 'I seem to have a talent for that, a kind of sixth sense that tells me when to buy and when to get out—it's fascinating, like an intricate board game played for very high stakes. So I've made a lot of money the past few years, more than is good for me, perhaps.'

'And you came back to Carmel.'

'If I hadn't, I wouldn't have met you... Roslin, if we keep on seeing each other, sooner or later we'll make love, you know that as well as I do.'

She said with a calmness that amazed her, 'I'll see that there's no pregnancy.'

'But what about the emotional side of it? That's not as easily avoided. Take a pill so you won't fall in love— the prescription's not available for that. For either of us.'

'You wouldn't just disappear without warning me?' she said, voicing a terror that had been with her for the last two weeks.

'No. But I can't promise I won't disappear.'

She said frankly, 'This has to be the strangest discussion I've ever had in my life. And the most unexpected.'

His smile was wry. 'It's called honesty.'

'You're scared, too, aren't you, Tyson?'

'I'm a man—I'm not supposed to be.'

Roslin managed a laugh. 'We're being honest, remember?'

'Yeah, I'm scared. Scared I'll find I need you. Scared I'll hurt you.'

'Scared you might be happy?' she asked with sudden insight.

'You see too much, Roslin.'

'We could risk it,' she murmured. 'You might discover happiness isn't so dreadful, after all.'

Tyson tore free of her. 'I must be a fool to even be thinking of it. You're ten years younger than me, you're a virgin; you couldn't be more different from those other women.'

'Of course I'm different. That's the whole point.'

But the strain of the scene was beginning to tell on her; she was unconsciously wringing her hands, and she was very pale. Tyson said abruptly, 'Let's give ourselves a couple of days to think about it. I'll come back then.'

For six years Roslin had disciplined herself towards one goal; but she knew two days was too long to wait for Tyson's decision. 'Tomorrow,' she replied. 'You'll know by tomorrow.'

'Sea-witch,' he said softly. As if he were indeed under a spell, he closed the gap between them and cupped her face in his hands, his fingers exquisitely gentle. 'I thought I knew myself until I met you,' he whispered, and kissed her with the same gentleness.

If he could hold on to that gentleness, she need not fear his decision. 'Tomorrow,' Roslin said.

But then Tyson's voice changed. 'You tear me apart,' he said, his hands tightening fractionally, his eyes clouding in the way she dreaded. 'Tomorrow,' he repeated, turned on his heel and left the room.

She did not want to listen to the stairs creak and the front door slam, sounds all too evocative of his departure in the middle of the night two weeks ago. She pushed the bench into the piano and closed the lid, her fingers tracing patterns in the dust. Tomorrow, she thought. Tomorrow...

CHAPTER NINE

THE hours passed with excruciating slowness, Roslin alternating between absolute certainty that Tyson would become both friend and lover, and an equal certainty that he would leave Carmel and she would never see him again. Depending on her mood, she played some of Schubert's more romantic compositions and some of Brahms's gloomier ones; and she vacuumed the house from top to bottom, including the room with the piano. She did not sleep well.

At ten o'clock the next morning the telephone rang. Roslin picked up the receiver as gingerly as if it were a deadly cobra and said faintly, 'Hello?' Tyson would not give his answer over the telephone . . . would he?

'Ah, Roslin. Colby speaking.'

The cobra turned into a garden snake. She was not fond of them, but they did not fill her with unreasoning terror. She said after the briefest of pauses, 'I wondered when you'd get in touch with me.'

'I thought I'd give you time to adjust to the bucolic life,' her uncle said smoothly. 'Get over the initial euphoria, as it were. I'm staying at the village inn. May I drop in some time today?'

Although his choice of day could not have been worse, she knew she had to see him before Tyson; if Tyson's decision was to leave Carmel, she would be in no shape to see anyone. 'Give me half an hour,' she said crisply.

'I look forward to seeing you in your new domain. Goodbye.'

Roslin plunked the receiver down, wondering why Colby always talked like a failed novelist, and ran upstairs. In her trunk she had included a businesslike grey dress with a white collar and cuffs for just such a visit.

She hauled it on, put on black pumps and grey stockings, and brushed her hair into a smooth chignon with a black velvet ribbon. Swiftly she applied make-up. Then she heard the dogs bark as a vehicle approached. He had not wasted any time.

When the knock came at the front door, she was checking her appearance in the mirror with the cherubs; Colby would despise that mirror, she knew. She opened the door, her smile a nicely judged blend of cordiality and self-assurance.

The man on the step was Tyson. Not Colby. A taut-jawed Tyson whose dark hair was ruffled by the breeze and whose grey eyes were as full of turmoil as she had ever seen them. He looked her up and down. 'You should never wear grey,' he said. 'You look as if you're in mourning.'

'Tyson, Colby's coming,' she gasped, 'and I can't handle both of you at once.'

His eyes narrowed. 'The mysterious uncle from Boston?'

'He's on his way now from the inn.' Roslin grimaced. 'He'll want me to go back, I know he will, and I'm not going.' Then she heard the distant sound of a car approaching. 'That's him now!'

'I'll come back once he leaves,' Tyson said. 'Stick to your guns, Roslin.' And he gave her an unexpected grin that lifted her spirits immeasurably.

No sooner was Tyson's van out of sight over the hill than a taxi appeared, Colby ensconced in the back seat. He alighted, wearing a three-piece pinstripe suit and carrying an umbrella against the scattered clouds in the sky, for Colby believed in being prepared and did not like surprises. Roslin knew her rebellion after the competition in Budapest had shocked him to the toes of his immaculate Italian shoes.

Escorted by Mutt and Jeff, he walked across the gravel towards her as the cab reversed and drove away. 'Hello,

Colby,' she said, and offered her cheek for his token kiss. 'Would you like to sit outdoors?'

This was naughty of her, for Colby disliked anything to do with nature, and Great-Aunt Mellicent's fecund, untidy flowerbeds, loud with the humming of bees, would not please him at all. So she was not surprised when he said, 'I'd rather see the house. Mellicent was never much of a housekeeper...I understand the roof leaks.'

Colby must have been in touch with the trustees. 'I'm getting it fixed,' Roslin responded, shooing the dogs away, then ushering him indoors and into the living-room, where the breeze wafted in the open window. 'May I get you a coffee?'

'Thank you, no. Are you planning to stay for the rest of the summer, Roslin?'

'I'm planning to stay indefinitely, Colby.'

He placed his umbrella precisely in line with the edge of the old Persian carpet and said, 'Is there a piano here?'

'Yes. I played it for the first time yesterday. It needs tuning.'

In genuine horror he said, 'You haven't practised until yesterday?'

She folded her hands in her lap so he could see the gleam of her long, pink fingernails. 'That's correct,' she said.

Colby bit back a hasty reply, smoothing his sleek, ash-blond hair. 'I see... You're too much of a professional to be unaware of the dangers inherent in such neglect.'

Roslin said nothing. She sat poised on the edge of her chair, not a hair out of place, her ankles crossed, her hands still in her lap. But inwardly she was quaking; she had jumped to Colby's tune for too many years to dismiss him lightly.

He looked at her with a mournful reproach that, hearteningly, reminded her of Jeff. 'Your parents,' he said softly. 'Have you forgotten them, Roslin?'

Although Roslin had known he would take that approach, she still winced from his question. 'Of course I haven't. But this has nothing to do with them, Colby.'

'Your mother was a very fine cellist. Your father was renowned as a musicologist. That you had an innate musical talent was a delight to them both.' His voice deepened and throbbed. 'As we know, tragically they met their deaths before they could fully appreciate the flowering of your talent. The talent is in your hands, Roslin. Quite literally in your hands. It is up to you not to disappoint them, to maintain their impeccable standards of musicianship, to rise to the top.'

His pale blue eyes looked quite overcome with his own rhetoric. Roslin said loudly, 'I can't rise to the top. Budapest proved that.'

'A temporary setback; one must expect such things in the competitive world of the concert pianist.' He leaned forward in his chair. 'I have good news for you. Brinmar will take you on as a pupil.'

David Brinmar was one of the top three teachers in the United States, who had groomed several successful contestants for the Tchaikovsky competitions in Moscow: Colby had achieved a coup. Roslin said, 'You'll have to tell him I have other plans.'

Colby gaped like a stranded fish. 'Brinmar? Tell *Brinmar* you have other plans? That's musical suicide, Roslin!'

It was her turn to lean forward. 'I'm through with the world of competitions—I haven't got whatever it takes to get to the top. I tried, Colby, you know better than anyone how hard I tried. But I cannot do it. I *will* not do it. You must accept that, because it's my final word.'

His nostrils were quivering. 'You're quitting. Giving up. At a time when the prize is in reach, you're throwing away all those years of hard work and dedication. You can't do that! I won't allow it.'

'You can't stop me. I have a house, and my allowance, and once I'm twenty-one I'll come into my parents' money. You had your years of controlling me—but they're over.'

He said bitterly, 'I'm glad your parents are dead, Roslin. I wouldn't want them to hear what you're saying to me today. What a terrible disappointment they would have found you.'

It was the cruellest thing he could have said. Roslin said in a stifled voice, 'Please, Colby—don't be like that.'

'The truth hurts, doesn't it?' Colby snapped. 'I shall inform Brinmar that you're giving up because you have neither the courage nor the fortitude to cope with the after-effects of Budapest. That, as you know, will finish you as far as a career as a concert pianist is concerned.'

'Good,' she said dully.

'I, also, am immensely disappointed in you,' he said pompously, and reached for his umbrella with an audible sniff. 'Quite apart from anything else, had I known you were to be so intransigent I would have asked the taxi to wait. Where is the telephone?'

'In the hall.'

She stood aside to let him pass, and waited as he called a cab. He was standing with rigid formality in the hall, the cherubs simpering at him. She heard herself cry, 'Why do we have to fight about this, Colby? So I'm not suited to be a concert pianist—it's not the end of the world! You're the only relative I have left, I'd like to think we could be friends.'

'Impossible,' her uncle said, adjusting his silk tie a fraction of an inch to the left. 'I devoted my life to your career, Roslin, only to have you throw those years in my face.'

'I didn't ask you to take over my career!'

'I saw it as my duty to my dead brother and his dear wife. I see now that I made a tactital error in judgement when I assumed you had the depth of character and the perseverance of your parents. I shall not make that mistake again.'

After that, there seemed nothing more to say. The taxi eventually arrived, the dogs barked, and Colby, without a backward look, departed. Roslin locked the door behind him. Then she climbed the stairs to her room and threw herself across the bed. Her eyes were burning with unshed tears, yet somehow she could not cry; his words had bitten too deep.

The doorbell rang. She heard it with one compartment of her mind and knew she could not possibly face Tyson now. Willing him to go away, neglecting to wonder how he had arrived so promptly, she pulled the pillow over her ears. She could see her parents as clearly as if they stood in front of her, her rumpled, genial father ransacking his study to find a manuscript he had lost, her mother bowed over her cello, practising. Her mother had practised for hours every day; her mother had been a concert cellist; her mother had not quit. In her mind's eye their faces seemed to turn away from her in sorrow and disappointment...

Tyson said strongly, 'You don't need a relative like that, Roslin.'

She jumped, for the voice had spoken from the doorway. Twisting on her side, she saw that Tyson was indeed standing at the door of her bedroom. She said foolishly, 'I locked the door.'

'I told you some time ago that this house is child's play to break into.'

'Why didn't the dogs bark?'

He gave her a smug smile. 'The dogs are my friends.'

She frowned, for some of the implications of both his appearance and his speech were sinking in. 'How did you get here so fast?'

'I never left.'

'You mean you listened? *Eavesdropped?*'

'At the living-room window, which was so obligingly open.'

'Tyson, that's immoral!'

He sat down on the end of the bed. 'No doubt. I wanted to know why you left Boston and why you had such a horror of control.' This time his smile was ironic. 'I sure found out. You're well rid of your Uncle Colby, Roslin. I had a very strong urge to leap through the window and poke him in the nose.'

Although his words were light, his eyes were watchful. Roslin said sharply, 'Some things can't be fixed by a poke in the nose—that would have been a stupid and irrelevant gesture.'

'Satisfying, though.'

She choked back a laugh that she knew could easily turn to tears. Spreading her hands, with their too-long nails, studying them as if she had never seen them before, she said, 'I did quit. He was right.'

'Why don't you tell me the whole story and let me be the judge of that?'

He was reclining across the end of the bed, leaning on one elbow. Roslin said evenly, 'First things first. What's your decision?'

He did not pretend to misunderstand her. 'The answer's yes,' he said. 'I want to risk the relationship... What's yours, Roslin?'

'Even after everything that you heard?'

'For pity's sake! I don't know how you stood him as long as you did. Answer the question, will you?'

He was swearing again; and he was afraid of her response. She said quietly, 'Oh, I didn't have to make a decision, I knew all along. The answer's yes for me, too.'

The air left Tyson's lungs in a long sigh. 'You had me worried,' he confessed. 'Figured you'd have better things to do with your time than fool around with a grown man who's as scared as if you were his first date.'

His admission broke through her haze of misery. Roslin reached out to touch his shoulder and said with simple truth, 'Please don't be scared, Tyson—I only want you to be happy.'

He brought his own hand up to cover hers; his voice was unsteady. 'Even in that dreary grey dress, I want to make love to you.'

'The dress was for Colby, not for you. And you can't.' she blushed. 'I haven't been to the drug-store.'

'We'll look after that this afternoon—I'll take you to Buckton. Tell me about Colby, Roslin.'

'Don't rush me,' she said in a thin voice, and she was not referring to Colby.

'Want to back out already?' Tyson said with a touch of cynicism that dismayed her.

'I don't want to back out at all. But neither do I want to feel that I have no say in the relationship,' Roslin answered roundly, deciding she did not really like this peculiar word relationship. What did it mean? A love-affair? A courtship? A one-night stand? She might have been wise to enquire before embarking upon it.

'It doesn't look as though we're going to stop fighting,' he remarked with a gleam in his eye.

'Did you really expect us to?' She added spontaneously, 'You're good for me—I was ready to cry my eyes out when Colby left.'

'So tell me about him.'

Having no notion where to start, she plunged straight in. 'My mother was Celia Cowper——'

'The cellist? So that's why the photograph on the mantel seemed familiar.'

'And my father was Bevan Hebb. He was a musicologist, specialising in the early Baroque period.'

Tyson said, a strange note in his voice, 'Distinguished antecedents you have.'

His own, of course, were not. Roslin bit her lip and said straightforwardly, 'They were good parents. My father was larger than life, a bear of a man, vague, jovial, obsessive—but unfailingly there if you needed him. My mother was away a lot on tour…the house used to come to life when she came home because she'd give parties and cook the most fabulous meals and fill the house with friends and song and laughter. They adored each other, and they surrounded me with love. They *were* delighted when they realised I had a talent for the piano.'

She had run out of words. Tyson said emotionlessly, 'You were very fortunate.'

'I don't think your upbringing was much like mine,' she ventured.

'Not much. What happened after they died, Roslin?'

She traced the pattern in the quilt with her finger. 'I couldn't believe they were dead... I was devastated. I threw myself into my music, because at least it gave me an outlet for my grief, and that's when Colby took over— he become my legal guardian, you see. Make your music a memorial to your parents, he said. Rise to the top, so their names will not be forgotten. Work, work, work, so you will be worthy of them.'

'And at fourteen you fell for that, hook, line and sinker.'

'For six years I fell for it. I did everything Colby told me. I had a tutor so I'd have more time for the piano, I practised for hours every day, I gave public performances and entered some of the minor competitions here and in Europe. I didn't know it at the time, but I was like a machine for the production of music.' Her eyes were faraway. 'But then Colby made three mistakes.'

'Budapest?'

'That came last. First, I had a series of lessons with Ferrolino in Italy about four months ago. He had five other pupils, one of whom, Aloysha, started flirting with me quite outrageously.' She added with a touch of defiance, 'It was fun.'

'I bet your uncle didn't think so.'

'He dragged me into every museum in Florence in the next three weeks, I swear—I saw enough marble busts to last a lifetime. But even Colby couldn't prevent me from talking with the others, and discovering just how limited my life was in comparison to theirs.'

'Mistake number two?'

'I was in a television show, "the making of a musician", you know the sort of thing. I suddenly realised how important my looks were to Colby; he was far more interested in my hairdo than my arpeggios. I'd become a saleable commodity.'

'The packaging of the product,' Tyson murmured.

'Very disconcerting when the product is you. Then came the competition in Budapest. Big-time stuff.'

'Beethoven's *Appassionata*?'

Roslin nodded. 'That was one of my pieces. I'd practised it until I could have played it in my sleep. I'd studied every nuance of dynamics and tempo.' Her mouth tightened. 'And what I realised about an hour before I was due to play was that I hated it ... I'd analysed all the life and beauty out of it. It was a dead piece of music.'

She shrugged. 'Even though this discovery terrified me, threw me completely off balance, I played the piece anyway. I came seventeenth out of the twenty-eight pianists. And afterwards I told Colby I'd never go in another competition in my life. That competing killed my joy in music.' Another shrug. 'Which was when I saw that he didn't even like me. Never had, I shouldn't think. Talk about growing up in a hurry.'

'He doesn't like anyone but himself,' Tyson said.

'The rest of the story you know—I had inherited this house, and once all the legalities were dealt with, I left Boston and came here.'

'And threw the key to the piano room into the brier patch.'

Her nail was now digging into the quilt. 'A natural enough reaction, I would have thought.'

'Are you going to get the piano tuned, Roslin?'

She had expected sympathy. She said tartly, '*I* don't know!'

'Chopin would appreciate it if you did.'

'I don't even know if I want to play any more,' she cried.

'Let's leave out the pernicious influence of your uncle——'

'Pernicious is the kind of word he'd use,' Roslin snapped.

Tyson grinned. 'I'm trying not to use cuss words, honeybunch.'

When he smiled at her like that, her heart melted. She said in a low voice, 'Did I let my parents down, Tyson?'

'No, Roslin—because you were too young and vulnerable to understand what was happening. But now you do understand. So what you do now is what counts.'

She should have known Tyson's character was too uncompromising for him to insult her with easy sympathy. She gulped. 'OK. I'm with you.'

He ticked off his fingers. 'You have a heritage of music. You had, six years ago, a genuine love of music. You're the seventeenth-best young pianist in the world—don't knock it. Finally, you have a choice to make.'

'I begin to see why you're no longer working in a mine.'

'Don't change the subject. Your first choice is to pursue the concert pianist route. You may never be top, but you sure could come close.'

Her response was swift and certain. 'I can't—it's not what I want to do.'

'You could teach.'

She frowned. 'Not yet. I don't know enough.'

'You could be an accompanist.'

Roslin sat up in a flash of nylon-clad legs; absently she hitched her skirt down. 'None of those is right. Do you know what I want to do, Tyson? I've never told anyone this, it sounds so pretentious...'

The strained look had left her face; her features glowed with life. 'Tell me,' he said.

'I want to compose. You don't know how often I hear melodies and phrases in my head, notes that echo and re-echo...but with Colby I didn't have the time or the energy to pursue them. Or the knowledge,' she added realistically. 'I'd have to go somewhere to study the principles of composition... I'd love to do that.'

'Then do it. Just don't bury yourself in Carmel to spite Colby.'

'I had to get away from him!'

'Sure you did. But now you're in danger of throwing away the baby with the bathwater.'

Roslin said ruefully, 'You sure tell it the way it is, don't you?'

'Fairy stories only happen in books, Roslin.'

She remembered the fairy-tales of her childhood, *Cinderella*, the *Sleeping Beauty*, and *Snow White*, and the handsome princes who had loved them. 'That's not true—you helped me slay a dragon today,' she said softly. Leaning forward, she kissed him full on the mouth.

With an inarticulate groan, Tyson took her in his arms, falling across her, devouring her with frantic, hungry kisses that took her by storm, his hands roaming her body with the same passionate urgency. And, because they were now committed to making love, he frightened her with his voracity; she felt like a small woodland creature encircled by a forest fire. Struggling against him, she gasped his name.

He grew still, burying his face in her neck. 'I'm sorry— I didn't mean to scare you,' he muttered.

She felt young and inadequate, unsure of how to deal with his compulsive energy, the fierceness of his demands. 'You took me by surprise,' she said weakly. 'It's all right.'

He raised his head. 'Can we go to Buckton this afternoon? There's a doctor there I can recommend.'

The flames were crackling at her back, Roslin thought wildly. Yet perhaps the only way to find the key to Tyson would be to make love with him; only then would he expose his vulnerabilities and needs, and open himself to tenderness. 'Yes,' she said.

'You'll have to change your outfit.'

Her chuckle sounded almost normal. 'You won't take me in my grey dress?'

'I will not.' His voice deepened. 'Change now, Roslin. Let me watch you.'

Colour flared in her cheeks. 'But——'

'Please . . . I won't touch you, I promise.'

Roslin knew that to undress in front of him would be a far more intimate act than those desperate kisses on the bed. Relationship, she decided, was a word that covered a lot of territory. But she also knew how the conversation on the bed had clarified both past and future, and that she owed Tyson a great deal for his stringent grasp of her situation. One good turn deserves another, she thought crazily, taking off her black pumps and placing them neatly on the floor of her wardrobe. Then, turning to face him, she began to undo the buttons down the front of the despised grey dress.

She had to twist to reach the zipper; and she could think of no graceful way to pull the dress over her head. When she emerged, her hair tousled, Tyson was watching her intently.

Her camisole and briefs were of palest green satin edged with lace; unable to face the burning intensity of his gaze, she hung the dress in the wardrobe, and with scant ceremony hauled the grey stockings down her legs. This, of course, necessitated leaning forward, which exposed her breasts. When she straightened, he said almost inaudibly, 'Your hair, Roslin—wear it loose.'

Her heart was racing and her bones seemed to have dissolved. If he were to take her in his arms now, she would not resist him; she wanted to walk into the heart of the fire. Raising her arms, her belly taut under the camisole, she unpinned her hair so that it tumbled free over her shoulders.

'You're so beautiful,' he breathed. 'When we make love I shall wrap you in your hair, like the sea-witch you are.' Then, with a speed that startled her, he swung round to the other side of the bed and stood up. 'I'd better get out of here, or I'll be going back on my word,' he said roughly. 'I'll wait for you downstairs and we'll go to Buckton.'

The stairs creaked as he descended. Roslin sat down heavily on the bed, which was still warm from his body. Tyson's ability to switch from rationality to passion and back again so quickly and so completely was frightening. It seemed inhuman. Too controlled. Too mechanical. And meanwhile she was left with her body aching and her emotions in turmoil. She was a fool to think that once they were in bed together he would change. He was thirty years old and he had never learned to love. Who was she to change that? And what would this so-called relationship cost her?

She had no answers to her own questions. She put on her flowered skirt and blouse and went downstairs to join him.

CHAPTER TEN

BY FOUR-THIRTY that afternoon Roslin had the small pink disc of pills in her bag and was waiting for Tyson in the bookshop. Bookshops were normally some of her favourite places. But too much had happened today; she had the beginnings of a headache and she felt very tired. When Tyson came into the store, she was thumbing through a paperback, the fluorescent lighting harsh on her face, her hair looking too heavy for the slender line of her neck. He came up beside her and said, 'Ready to go home?'

She looked up at him, for a moment seeing him as if he were a stranger to her. The restless grey eyes, the thatch of dark hair, the broad-shouldered, narrow-hipped body, all seemed infused with energy even when he was standing still, the room too small to contain him. How could she hope to teach this man anything about love, she who had only known the love of parents and had never loved a man?

'What's wrong, Roslin?'

She suppressed a shiver. 'Tired, I guess.'

'Come on, we'll go home and I'll cook supper for you.'

And then what? she wondered. 'I have to pick up a few groceries in Carmel,' she said.

Tyson went to the post office while she bought the groceries; so she was alone when she came face to face with Liza over the fish counter. Roslin had asked for cod, because her money was dwindling rather rapidly, while Liza was ordering jumbo shrimps and scallops. Without preamble Liza said, 'I gather from Amy and Annabel that you are no longer seeing Tyson.'

'That's changed,' Roslin said baldly.

'Changed? What do you mean?'

The throbbing at Roslin's temples was now a full-fledged headache, and the smell of fish was making her feel sick. 'Tyson and I have decided to explore the possibilities of relationship,' she said, in a sentence worthy of Colby.

Liza was openly glaring at her. 'What precisely does that mean?'

You tell me, thought Roslin, clutching the plastic bag of soft white fillets. 'Perhaps it would be more appropriate if you asked Tyson,' she suggested.

'Tyson informed me before I went to Boston that he and I would no longer be dating. I don't care to ask him.' Liza tossed her cap of blonde hair.

'So did you date anyone else in Boston?'

'What business is that of yours?'

'Liza,' Roslin said patiently, 'you would never have married Tyson because, no matter how much money he's made, he's still the son of the local drunk and the cleaning lady—that kind of thing matters to you and your friends. You wouldn't have done it, I'd swear on fifty pounds of shrimp you wouldn't. The only reason you're upset is that Tyson did the rejecting, not you.' She was warming to her theme. 'Tyson had enough rejection as a boy; surely you can allow him his turn for once? On top of which, you're a beautiful woman who should have no trouble replacing him with someone more suitable.' She smiled. 'Someone born to jumbo shrimps.'

Liza looked down her patrician nose. 'You've got it all figured out.'

'Admit I'm right,' Roslin coaxed with another smile.

'I do like shrimps,' Liza said defiantly.

'On a silver spoon.'

'I suppose you're right.' For the first time in their acquaintance Liza smiled at Roslin, a rather grudging smile, but a smile nevertheless. 'I wish you luck with Tyson,' she said sardonically. 'I've known him since he was five years old and I've yet to meet the person who could handle him... and I'm sure that over the years women other than you and me have tried.' With another smile, this one full of mockery, she added, 'Goodbye, Roslin,' and headed for the cash registers.

Why do I start these conversations? Roslin wondered, flinching away from the bulging eye of a scrod laid out on the crushed ice. All Liza has done is confirm my doubts.

She added aspirin to her list of purchases, paid for them, and left the store. Tyson was waiting for her in the van. As she buckled her seat-belt he said, 'You look worse.'

She felt worse. 'I've got a headache,' she muttered.

'The classic excuse.'

In a flash of temper Roslin said, 'It's got nothing to do with you—it was seeing Colby, and thinking about Budapest. I don't think you understand what that competition did to me—I'll never forget how I felt afterwards! I'd lived and breathed music since the day I was born. I'd formed my life around one goal for six years. And then in Budapest I discovered that I'd grown to hate the very thing I loved.' She shivered. 'I was left with nothing... It was the most terrifying sensation, as if the foundation of my whole personality had been whipped from under me and I was suspended in a void.'

'So you ran away.'

'A useless exercise, I see that now—there are pianos wherever you go.'

'Roslin, give yourself a break. Practise when you feel like it. Play for your own pleasure. If you hear a tune in your head, fool around with it. But don't make a machine out of yourself.'

'Freedom,' she whispered.

'You in the driver's seat. Not Colby or your parents. You.'

She leaned back in the seat, closing her eyes. 'Let's go home.'

When they got there, Tyson carried the groceries into the kitchen and began unpacking them. His back to her, he said brusquely, 'Would you rather I left now?'

Roslin had been searching for the aspirin. Staring at his back, which was about as revealing as the door of the refrigerator, she said irritably, 'What do *you* want to do?'

He suddenly turned on her. 'How should I know? You sure don't look as though you want company.'

The throbbing had become a band squeezing her forehead. 'I have a headache, I keep telling you!'

'So you don't need me.'

She clutched the edge of the counter. 'You've got it wrong—you don't want me to need you,' she retorted, and knew that at some level she had said the truth, for Tyson looked as startled as if she had slapped him.

There was a dead silence. Then he grated, 'Just what do you mean by that?'

'You only want an affair with me, Tyson—no strings attached, no emotional involvement,' Roslin said incoherently. 'And here I am ruining it because I've got a headache and I feel lousy because Colby's visit upset me, and I don't feel like going to bed with you because I'm scared to death of doing that, and so what do you want to do? You want to run. Get out of here as fast as you can in case I make demands on you that you don't want to meet.' Her eyes seemed to be swimming with tears. She finished raggedly, 'And now I'm really going to add to your day by bursting into tears like a typical hysterical female, and for goodness' sake get *lost*!'

She grabbed for the box of Kleenex on the counter and blew her nose. Tyson said with brutal truth, 'I've never allowed anyone to make demands on me—I told you I've always been a loner.'

Roslin glared at him over the tissues. 'I won't allow you to be a loner—not with me.'

His eyes narrowed. 'I'd like to know how you plan on changing me.' Then he added in a voice Roslin had not heard him use before, '*Are* you scared of making love with me?'

Her forehead felt as if it was expanding and contracting. 'Yes,' she mumbled.

'Great start to the relationship.'

'I'm beginning to hate that word!'

'You're not the only one... The only advice I can offer is to take two aspirin and go to bed. Alone.'

'Which will allow you to leave with a clear conscience.' She gave him a dirty look.

He met her look with one equally unfriendly. 'I'll give you a call tomorrow.'

Roslin hated being alone when she had a headache. But she would not have admitted that now for all the money Tyson had offered her for the house. 'Fine,' she said. 'Goodnight.'

She heard his footsteps retreat along the hall. She had expected to spend the evening losing her virtue. But Tyson no longer seemed the slightest bit interested in attacking it.

Roslin awoke clear-headed and in a militant mood. Part of her headache, she decided, had been nothing to do with Budapest, but had stemmed from the stress of her relationship—that word again—with Tyson. If he ran from her demands, from the reality of a relationship, he would either have to change, or she would have to let him go. Because she refused to be less than real.

When he phoned today she would tell him so.

She went downstairs and let the dogs out. Then she showered and washed her hair, put on jeans and a cotton shirt, and headed for the kitchen to make breakfast. A robin was patrolling the lawn for worms, leaving tiny tracks in the dew, its head cocked as it approached the bronzed petals of the wallflowers that nodded under the window; admiring its concentration, Roslin plugged in the coffee-maker, trying to conjure up a strategy that would break through Tyson's reserve to the man within. Because letting him go did not seem such a great idea.

Then the dogs set up a hideous barking, and the robin flew away. Peering through the back door, Roslin could see the two of them leaping and pawing at the foot of the largest maple beyond the driveway. A porcupine, she thought. They've treed a porcupine and they want me to go out and congratulate them.

She unlocked the back door and crossed the gravel to the maple. However, the creature wrapped around a branch half-way up the tree was not a porcupine but a cat, a black cat that hissed impartially at the dogs and Roslin, its malevolent green eyes glowing, its bushy tail lashing at the leaves. 'Well,' said Roslin, 'where did you come from?'

The cat's answer was unprintable. Roslin restrained Mutt from trying to scale the tree and took Jeff by the collar, dragging both of them, much against their wishes, into the back porch. Then she went outside again. The cat, far from being grateful, had climbed higher in the tree; it was so thin and unkempt that Roslin concluded it must be a stray. She fetched a dish of milk and placed it under the tree.

Fifteen minutes later the cat was still anchored in the crook of two branches, but was now mewing so piercingly that Roslin knew she had to do something. She fetched Great-Aunt Mellicent's ladder, told herself she was not really afraid of heights, and crawled up the wooden rungs one by one until she could clasp the trunk and hitch herself into the tree. 'Come on, Blackie,' she coaxed. ''You can stay at my house until I find out if you're lost . . . nice Blackie.'

Blackie hissed and inched a little further up the branch. 'I'll feed you tuna,' Roslin cajoled.

The green eyes glowered at her. Then Roslin made the mistake of looking down. The ground was a very long way away, and the ladder looked exceedingly frail. She embraced the trunk with fervour and in the early morning silence heard the purr of an approaching engine.

She was somehow not surprised when Tyson's grey camper drove over the hill and parked by the house. As he got out, she called, 'It's not a pure white steed, but it'll do.'

His head swung round. His hands in his pockets, he strolled over to the maple. 'Good morning, Roslin,' he said.

Her strategy fell into place as neatly as if she had planned it. 'Tyson,' she said, 'I'm not proud. I'm perfectly willing to admit that right now I need you.'

'Three more feet'll do it.'

'I'm terrified of heights. Besides, the cat's not convinced it wants rescuing.'

'But you do.'

Still hugging the trunk, she managed to bob a curtsy. 'Please, Sir Galahad.'

'Are you planning to add that mangy ball of fur to your menagerie?'

The cat growled. 'I feel it might be more of a match for Bradleigh than Mutt,' she said thoughtfully.

'Get down, Roslin, and I'll climb the tree for you,' Tyson said in a resigned voice.

Hurriedly, before she could lose her nerve, Roslin went on, 'I wasn't strictly truthful with you last night, Tyson—I hate being alone when I have a headache. I needed you to stay, but I didn't say so.'

'That's why I'm here so early—to apologise for not staying.'

Roslin slithered down the trunk, her right foot finding the top rung of the ladder. Only then did she look over her shoulder. 'Say that again.'

'I should have stayed—I'm sorry.'

She gave him her most generous smile. 'You're forgiven,' she said, and started down the ladder.

Tyson grasped the uprights to steady the ladder, so when she reached the ground she was standing in the circle of his arms. Wide-eyed, she remarked, 'Another theory's just bitten the dust.'

A smile glimmered in his eyes. 'What theory, honeybunch?'

'That black cats bring bad luck. Kiss me good morning, Tyson.'

'Bossy, aren't you?' he murmured, and kissed her with a mixture of mastery and tenderness that entranced her.

The cat began to howl in a dedicated way. Roslin pulled free and said breathlessly, 'I think it's a prude.'

'I think it's a damned nuisance,' Tyson responded, trailing kisses down her cheek.

Trying very hard to remember her strategy, Roslin murmured, 'But I do think it wants rescuing.'

He let go of her shoulders, his grey eyes still sparked with passion as he glanced upwards. 'I hope you're right.'

Tyson was plainly not scared of heights, scaling the tree with an agility Roslin envied. She waited until he had almost reached the cat, his feet braced on a sturdy limb, before she removed the ladder, laying it on the ground. Then she said, 'Tyson, I have a request to make.'

Through the canopy of leaves he looked down at her; she was tapping the rungs with one foot. 'Do you, now?' he said equably.

'You'll need the ladder to get down—it's too far to jump.'

'Blackmail, Roslin?'

'Coercion,' she said gravely. 'All you have to do is repeat after me, "I need your help, Roslin"... Got that? Even an abbreviated version will do: "Roslin, I need you".'

'And if I choose not to?'

She tilted her head to one side. 'It could be a long morning. I wouldn't put it past the cat to go into attack mode, would you? Its name is Blackie, by the way.'

'I hope your compositions show more originality than the names of your pets,' Tyson replied. 'Come here, Blackie...come on down.'

The cat, to Roslin's annoyance, obeyed instantly, settling itself on Tyson's shoulder. He yelped as it dug its claws into his shirt. Then he said, grinning at her, 'Roslin, I need to be rescued from a cat that's kneading me...will that do?'

She put her hands on her hips. 'Cut out the puns. "Roslin, I need you".'

'Roslin, I need you...ouch!'

'There—that wasn't so difficult, was it?' Roslin said jubilantly.

'The ladder, Miss Hebb.'

She leaned it against the tree and supported it as Tyson and the cat descended the trunk. Six rungs from the bottom, the cat launched itself from Tyson's shoulder and leaped to the ground, where it raced for the nearest patch of bushes and crouched, glaring at them both and muttering under its breath. Tiny patches of blood appeared on Tyson's T-shirt.

'Tyson, you're hurt!'

He put the back of his hand to his forehead, swayed on his feet and gasped, 'Roslin, I need you.'

She was torn between laughter and concern. 'Think what that cat could do to Bradleigh.'

He daubed at his shoulder. 'Bradleigh's better padded than I am. In any stories I've ever read about knights of old, the beauteous maiden didn't stand around and giggle while the poor knight bled to death.'

She gave him an impulsive hug. 'Come to the kitchen, Sir Galahad, and I'll ply you with coffee.'

'And what about Blackie?'

'He's just shy,' Roslin said optimistically. 'If we go inside, I bet he'll drink the milk.'

'Vindictive would be a more accurate word,' Tyson said feelingly, rubbing his shoulder as he followed Roslin across the driveway. 'I expect sympathy with my coffee.'

In the kitchen Roslin poured the coffee, then insisted on daubing an antiseptic ointment on the claw marks in Tyson's shoulder; he had removed his shirt, and his skin

was cool over the flow of bone and muscle. She got rather
more ointment on him than was necessary and managed
to drop the cap on the floor, whereupon she and Tyson
bumped heads when they both reached for it at once.
Passing the cap to her, he pulled his shirt on and said
with a return of the grimness she had come to dread, 'I
can't stay long—some of us work for a living.'

Once again her virtue was not to be assailed. Trying
to sound as if his departure was a matter of complete
unimportance, Roslin said, 'Are you supposed to be
standing on the floor of the stock market yelling your
offers and waving bits of tape?'

'I should be sitting in front of my computer plugged
into the phone,' he corrected her. 'Five o'clock most
mornings that's where I am.'

'Do you enjoy your work?'

He took a gulp of coffee. 'I'm thinking of some
changes—maybe set up a foundation and oversee it. Put
some of the money to good use.'

'What sort of use?' Roslin asked, curious.

'Oh, street kids, runaways, something like that,' Tyson
said vaguely, and drained his mug. 'Do you want to go
to one of the offshore islands this afternoon? Take a
picnic?'

He could not have expressed more clearly his aversion
to discussing runaways. 'I'd like that,' Roslin said
politely.

'I'll make the arrangements and look after the food—
I'll pick you up around three.' He gave her a brief smile.
'Good luck with Blackie.'

As he left the kitchen, she knelt to search in the cupboard for a can of tuna with which to begin the taming
of Blackie. Blackie, she was certain, would be an easier
proposition than Tyson.

By four o'clock that afternoon Roslin and Tyson were
scudding across the bay in a borrowed power-boat, the
sun dancing on the waves, the wind moulding Roslin's

shorts and halter-top to her body. Tyson was at the tiller, wearing shorts and sneakers and nothing else. She gave him a smile of pure pleasure and shouted over the roar of the motor, 'You know what? Carmel is a very claustrophobic little town.'

'Are you only just realising that?'

'I think you were smart to get out when you did.'

He said abruptly, 'I've put the house on the market.'

Feeling as though the sun had gone behind a cloud, Roslin faltered, 'When are you leaving?' He had not promised not to leave, she remembered. He had only promised to warn her.

'Not before autumn.'

'And what about us? This...relationship we keep talking about?'

'We'll know by then, don't you agree, Roslin?'

As out of her depth as if he had flung her overboard into the chill blue ocean, she looked away from him, and with the shock of a wave slapping her in the face recognised the truth. She knew already. She was in love with him.

She sat very still on the slatted wooden bench, staring unseeingly at the horizon. She loved Tyson.

No current of joy followed her discovery. Tyson did not love her; he was fighting against the very emotions she craved for him to feel. He wanted to make love to her...or at least she thought he did. He admired her musical ability. He quite possibly liked her. But he was determined not to fall in love with her, and equally determined not to need her.

He called out, 'That's the island we're going to—the one that's just come into sight behind the larger one. The friend who loaned me the boat owns both of them.'

The tiny island, capped with spruce trees and laced with foam, would normally have delighted Roslin. But the weight of her discovery held her pinioned, much as Tyson's weight had pinioned her to the bed; whatever freedom she had found by fleeing from Colby she had forfeited.

Tyson drove the boat up on the beach, anchoring it there. They went for a swim that was both brief and active because the water was so cold, then stretched out on the sand, Tyson's towel a careful distance away from hers. He fell asleep. Roslin pulled on her shorts and sneakers and explored the island, finding an old foundation at the far end with gnarled apple trees and an ancient lilac bush, where goldfinches cavorted in the thistles, the males lemon-yellow, the females drab olive. She felt rather a drab olive herself, thought Roslin. This island, so beautiful and remote, was a perfect place to make love. And where was Tyson? Asleep.

She skipped rocks on the surface of the water for a while, then wandered back along the shore. Tyson was unloading the picnic from the boat. 'Hungry?' he asked.

Sand and salt crystals were caught in the tangled hair on his chest; his swimming trunks were brief enough to leave little to the imagination. She thought of walking up to him, brushing away the sand and saying, 'Yes. For you.' She did not do it.

As they ate, she chattered away about everything she had seen at the other end of the island, and in return Tyson talked about some of his travels as a young man. While he did not speak about life in Carmel, he was still sharing some of his experiences with her; building companionship, Roslin thought stoutly. Companionship was very important. After all, she was sure he wanted her. She must just be patient.

He left her at the front door that evening. The next day they went blueberry-picking in a field full of other people, and the day after to Popham Beach, which on a hot summer's day was far from deserted. On each occasion she was deposited at her door. The following day Tyson phoned to say the commodities market was behaving abnormally, and the next day phoned her from

New York, where he stayed for four more days. The Thursday he returned, he arranged to take her for dinner.

Roslin's first thought when she saw him was how handsome he looked in his light grey suit, white shirt and raw silk tie; her second that he looked very tired. She had spent the better part of the afternoon getting ready, her hair in an elaborate coil, her tailored dress, in deep blue linen, subtly emphasising the hidden blues in her eyes and the curves of her figure. Tyson said flatly, 'I hadn't thought you could possibly be as beautiful as I remembered you.'

She closed the gap between them, rested her hand on his sleeve and said deliberately, 'That's the first personal remark you've made to me since the day I had the headache.'

'Is it?' He gently removed her hand, said, 'I can't kiss you, I'll ruin your make-up...shall we go?'

Her eyes glittered, for patience could last only so long. 'I recall saying to you, in a rash moment, that I would not allow you to be a loner. What do I have to do to gain your attention? Drop a piano on your toe?'

'You always have my absolute and undivided attention,' Tyson said.

She glared at him. 'Oh, yeah? You were in a great hurry to get me to the drugstore. I'm beginning to think I wasted my money.'

For a moment raw emotion broke through his composure. 'You also said to me, the day of the famous headache, that you were afraid of me. Scared to death was the phrase you used. How the hell do you think that made me feel?'

She was obscurely comforted to hear him swearing. 'Afraid of making love. Not afraid of you.'

'There's a difference?'

She did not deign a reply. 'I really hate feeling like your sister. Or a blind date you can't wait to get rid of.'

'Roslin,' Tyson said, raising one brow, 'I haven't eaten since six o'clock this morning, I had to bribe the *maître d'* to get the reservation, and if we're late we'll never get another one—do you think we could continue this—er—discussion after dinner?'

'Only if you give me a hug.'

A smile tugged at the corner of his mouth. 'You're being very assertive.'

'I promise not to get lipstick on your shirt.'

Tyson put his arms around her and almost lifted her off the ground in a bone-cracking hug. Then he released her. She said blankly, 'You really *are* glad to see me.'

'Of course I am,' he said shortly.

'You keep me at arm's length and give me these inscrutable looks and yet somehow I'm supposed to know that you're devoured by passion? Pooh,' said Roslin.

He laughed. 'The reservation's for eight, honeybunch.'

She stamped her elegantly shod foot. 'Don't call me that! And before we go, admit you could be the teeniest bit irritating to a female who's intent on getting past the macho image to the man within.'

'I claim the fifth amendment.'

Roslin raised her eyes heavenwards, took his arm and said, 'Come along, we'd better get to this restaurant before you pass out from starvation or exhaustion or both, and you can tell me about New York on the way. Have the commodities been duly reprimanded for misbehaving?'

They had reached the van. Tyson opened her door. His hand resting on the handle, he said in a strained voice, 'Nothing's changed for me—nothing. I still can't sleep at night for wanting you.'

Not for the first time, he had knocked her completely off balance. Wanting to weep, Roslin said, 'I want you, too.'

He brushed her cheek with his lips. 'Then we'll be all right,' he said.

The restaurant was in Blue Haven and was surrounded by a garden where Nicotiana and honeysuckle scented the air. The food was exquisitely prepared, and to her surprise Roslin did full justice to it. But all through the meal she was aware of undercurrents. She found herself studying Tyson's hands as he ate, the lean fingers with their well-kept nails, the strong tendons in the wrist; she thought of those hands on her body and trembled inwardly. When he raised his glass in a toast, his eyes seemed to caress her features as palpably as if he had actually stroked them. Their knees had a tendency to meet under the table.

Yet they did not rush the meal; and when they left the restaurant and stepped into the velvet, fragrant darkness Tyson said, 'Why don't we walk down to the wharf?'

He had put his arm around Roslin's shoulder; the scent of honeysuckle would always recall for her an unsettling mixture of security, panic and love. They strolled down the hill towards the black gleam of water where schooners and yawls, brightly lit, were anchored offshore, laughter and snatches of song drifting landward. Noisier songs burst from the tavern by the wharf; there was a constant traffic at the doorway.

They went to the very end of the wharf, watching a dinghy row out to a yacht strung with Chinese lanterns. 'It looks like something out of a movie,' Roslin murmured.

But Tyson's attention had been deflected. 'What's that?' he demanded.

'I don't——'

But he had left her to cross to the stairs on the other side of the wharf, stairs that were shrouded in darkness. Roslin hurried after him. Three men were scuffling on the steps, their raucous voices with an undertone of cruelty. 'What's going on?' Tyson said sharply.

Roslin leaned over the railing. Cringing in the midst of the three was an old man wearing an overcoat and a knitted cap; she saw one man land a kick at the old man's knees, and gave an indignant shout. But Tyson was leaping down the stairs. He hauled one of the men off bodily, throwing him against the pilings of the wharf, then said to the remaining two, 'Get lost, unless you want to get hurt.'

It did not seem to have occurred to him that he was out-numbered three to one and hampered by his tailored suit; the civilised clothes, on the contrary, made him look all the more dangerous. His fists were clenched and he was balanced on the balls of his feet, as volatile as an explosive. The first man picked himself up and scrambled up the steps. The other two edged around Tyson, giving him as wide a berth as they could without falling in the inky water. They were young, Roslin saw, and, like most bullies, intent on self-preservation.

The old man straightened, hiccuped, and said blearily, 'That wus real nice of you.'

Tyson said tersely, 'I'd better help you up the steps.'

The old man lurched to the top of the stairs, humming a little tune to himself, then said, as Tyson dropped his elbow, 'Gimme a dollar, would ya, boss? Long time since I had a proper bite to eat.'

Tyson said, 'I'll take you to the café up the street and arrange a twenty-dollar credit for you with the cashier.'

'But ya can't even get a beer there,' the old man protested. 'T'ain't licensed.'

'That's right,' said Tyson.

'C'mon, boss, a buck'll do,' the old man whined.

'No,' Tyson said implacably.

The old man hiccuped again. 'A cursh on yer mother 'n' yer grandmother,' he snarled, and staggered off down the street.

So much for gratitude, thought Roslin, shaken more than she would have cared to admit by this encounter. Tyson was rubbing his hands down the sides of his suit, as if the contact had soiled him. She walked to the head of the steps and said, 'Why wouldn't you give him the dollar?'

'So he could head straight for the tavern?' Tyson answered coldly.

'You don't know he would have done that.'

'I know.'

'How do you know, Tyson?' she said in deliberate challenge.

He turned to face her, the lines hard-bitten into his face. 'Let's not play games, Roslin—someone in Carmel must have enlightened you about my parentage.'

'I've been waiting for you to tell me yourself.'

He said violently, 'I couldn't leave him down there to be shoved in the water by those louts—but I was damned if I'd give him money to spend on rotgut, either.'

They were standing a foot apart. Like sparring partners, she thought. 'Did he remind you of your father?'

'Yes, Roslin, he did. Next question?'

'You're not making this any easier!' she cried.

'I would have thought the message was clear that I don't want to talk about my father.'

'I think it's high time you did,' she retorted, her cheeks flushed with emotion.

He grabbed her arm. 'Let's get out of here.' She saw that they were no longer alone on the wharf and, as she had no desire to entertain the revellers with her opinions on Tyson's reticence, she suffered him to lead her to the van. But once they were inside with the doors shut she said, 'I think you should——'

'Lay off, Roslin!'

She sat in a simmering silence all the way home, her brain working overtime. The dogs came gambolling to meet the van, tails wagging. No revellers here, thought Roslin. No witnesses. Only two dogs who should be used to her and Tyson fighting by now. She said calmly, 'When I was in the cellar the other day I discovered Great-Aunt Mellicent's stock of brandy—my father would heartily have approved of her taste. Why don't you come in and test it with me? Just to make sure it's still all right?'

Tyson raked his fingers through his hair. 'Look, I'm not in the mood for small talk in front of the fire.'

It was not small talk she had in mind. 'I promise I won't light the fire. One brandy and you can go home.'

She could almost see his good manners struggling with his desire to be alone. His manners won. 'All right,' he said stiffly, and got out of the van.

Roslin had noticed before that Tyson was in the habit of leaving the keys in the ignition. Leaning over very casually, she pocketed them. Then she too got out of the van. As her feet scrunched in the gravel, the sound exaggerated by the stillness of the night, the bunch of keys dug into her hip.

CHAPTER ELEVEN

As ROSLIN walked towards the house, the dogs leaped about her feet. Unlocking the front door, she said, 'Jeff's getting positively frisky. One of these days he's actually going to smile at me, I'm sure...but I still haven't been able to coax Blackie into the house. Have a seat, Tyson, and I'll get the brandy.'

She had put it in one of the kitchen cupboards. After tucking his keys behind the vegetable oil, she carried the brandy into the dining-room, where she got two snifters. Tyson was standing in front of the fireplace in the living-room; he raised his brows when he saw the label on the bottle, but made no comment. Roslin poured the amber liquid with the care it deserved, then passed him his glass. 'Cheers,' she said.

Brandy was not her favourite drink, but she had to admit it had a kick like a mule. She took another sip and said into the silence Tyson seemed disinclined to break, 'I promised not to make small talk in front of the fire. But I didn't promise not to fight, Tyson.'

He swirled the brandy in the snifter, which was cupped in his hands. 'Then, despite this admirable brandy, I shall have to leave.'

Roslin said with deliberate provocation, 'I know your father was the local drunk and that he used to hit you. I know your mother cleaned houses for people like Liza, and that by some of the righteous residents of Carmel she might have been considered promiscuous.' Her eyes flashed with emotion. 'Do you think it makes the slightest difference to me? Or do you think I'm a snob and that's why you won't talk about them?'

Tyson cracked the snifter down on the mantel so hard, she was surprised the glass did not shatter. 'A charming

end to the evening—congratulations,' he said. Then he
headed for the door.

Roslin said, conscious of her heart racing in her breast,
'I hid your car keys.'

Tyson whirled to face her so fast that she jumped.
'You little bitch!'

Her hands and feet felt as cold as ice. 'You opted for
the relationship, Tyson—this is part of it.'

He was advancing on her, his eyes blazing with rage,
and with the sickness of real fear she thought that the
violence she had glimpsed on the wharf was about to be
turned on her. Steeling herself to stand her ground,
knowing that if he left now she had lost him forever, she
said, 'Where did you get that scar over your eye?'

He stopped dead and snarled, 'My father pushed me
down the stairs. He was, of course, drunk.'

Roslin groped for the nearest chair, for her legs were
trembling. 'I thought that was what happened,' she said.

'Then I hope you're satisfied.'

She forgot about sitting down. 'Oh, stop it, Tyson!
You keep telling me I'm different from anyone you've
ever known—so if I'm different, tell me what it was like
to be the son of those parents, growing up an outcast
in the village of Carmel. Because you've never told
anyone else, have you?'

'And what if I don't want to?'

'Then you've got a long walk home.'

He took her by the wrist. 'I could make you tell me
where the keys are.'

She said stonily, 'But you won't—that's not your style.'

'How well you know me, Roslin,' he sneered. Suddenly he yanked her towards him, so that they stood
chest to chest. 'Well enough to take me into your bed?
Because that was the original plan for the evening, wasn't
it?'

Her eyes were dark pools of midnight-blue and the
pulse was fluttering at the base of her throat. 'Not when
you're behaving like this.'

'Going back on your word? That's not your style, Roslin.'

Hating him and loving him in equal measure, she announced, 'If we go to bed, it's to make love—not to shift the battlefield from downstairs to upstairs.'

Some of the anger faded from Tyson's face. 'You're a real fighter, aren't you? You won't back down.'

'That's because I'm fighting for us,' Roslin replied with commendable lightness. 'For this nebulous thing we're calling a relationship.' And forbore to add that for her it was not nebulous at all.

He let go of her, pacing over to the window. 'You're either extremely brave or extremely foolhardy,' he said.

Her knees were trembling again. Bracing herself against the armchair, almost certain she had won, she said, 'Tell me what it was like, Tyson.'

He was staring out into the darkness, his shoulders hunched. He said emotionlessly, 'Not enough food, because my father drank most of my mother's earnings. A tar-paper shack in the woods outside town with old cars lying all over the yard because he planned, some day, to start a used parts business...the day just never arrived. Second-hand clothes that people gave to my mother because they were sorry for her...one of the first fights I got into at school was with Bradleigh when he recognised the jacket I was wearing as one of his and decided to call the whole school's attention to it...I lost that fight, and quite a lot more. I was small for my age in those days.'

Roslin made an inarticulate sound of sympathy. 'So that's why this property seemed like paradise to you.'

'Of course.' Tyson turned his head, lines scoring his face. 'I wasn't a battered child, I don't want you to think that—my dad could be rough when he was drunk, but he rarely caused real harm. What was worse, I think, was the total lack of love in that house. When I was born my mother might have loved him, but by the time I was seven or eight I'd watched any kindness or caring

be worn down to bitterness and resentment. Obliterated.
They didn't love each other—they stayed together from
habit as much as anything—and I never had much evi-
dence that they loved me.'

Roslin said with a careful absence of emotion, 'What
happened when you'd lose a fight? Would your mother
hug you and try to make it better?'

'I don't remember either of them ever hugging me.
Or each other, for that matter.' Again Tyson turned his
head to gaze into the night. 'I don't like talking about
it, Roslin,' he said. 'What's the use? It's over and done
with, they're both dead, and anything I say sounds like
a bid for sympathy.'

'Yet it's marked you for life,' she replied. 'So it's not
over.'

He did not reply. When she crossed the room, tentatively taking him by the sleeve, he jerked away from
her. Her hand fell to her side, her eyes darkening with
the pain of rejection. He had told her his story, she
thought numbly. How naïve she had been to imagine
that the telling would be its own cure, that years of pri-
vation could be undone in five minutes.

The silence stretched on until Roslin's nerves were at
the screaming point. She said with the courage of desperation, 'It's never too late to learn to love, Tyson. You
didn't have good role models as a child, but that doesn't
mean you can't change as an adult. And I know you
can be gentle and caring. I've seen it.'

He shook his head. 'It is too late—I know it is.
Anyway, the gap between my background and yours is
unbridgeable.'

'Were my parents living, I would be proud to take you
home to them,' she declared. 'They would have liked
you, I'm convinced of it.'

'You live in a fairy-tale world, Roslin. A world of
happy endings.'

So she had lost. As exhausted as if she had run ten miles, Roslin said despairingly, 'I don't believe that happiness is unattainable.'

When Tyson turned around, he must have seen the defeated slump of her shoulders and the misery in her face. His jawline tightened. He took her by the wrist, his fingers biting like a manacle. 'Let's go upstairs,' he said.

Taken by surprise, trying to quell an upsurge of hope, Roslin searched his features for clues to his feelings. The anger was gone from his face, but she could not have said what, if anything, was in its place. He was waiting for her response, she did know that; he would not force her up the stairs. 'I didn't think you wanted to,' she whispered.

'I can't bear to see you so unhappy.'

Feeling as if she were making one of the most momentous decisions of her life, yet knowing that in one sense she had no choice at all, Roslin said prosaically, 'All right.'

Something flickered in his eyes. He put his arm around her waist and led her up the stairs; the seventh step and the fourth creaked as they always did. She turned on the lamp beside her bed and then immediately wished she had not, for it bathed the room in far too much light and she had no idea how they were to go about this.

Tyson said calmly, 'Haven't you any candles?'

'There's a package for emergencies in the bathroom cupboard.'

'From the look on your face, this is an emergency,' he said wryly. 'Go get one, Roslin.'

She fled to the bathroom, saw her white-faced reflection in the mirror, grabbed a candle and the matches, and went back into the bedroom. Tyson had taken off his jacket and tie.

Roslin put the candle in its wrought-iron holder on the dresser and tried to light a match. After two failed attempts, during which she burned her finger, Tyson took

the box from her and lit the candle. 'Your hands are
like ice,' he said, sounding almost gentle. 'Take your
clothes off and get into bed—I'll warm you.'

Hurriedly she switched off the lamp. He was now
lining up his shoes on the floor by the chair and stripping
off his socks, more like a husband of ten years than a
man driven by passion, she thought wildly, deciding she
must have been crazy to have hidden his keys; she was
the one who had instigated this. His hands moved to the
top button on his shirt. Turning her back on him, she
unzipped her dress and hauled it over head, careless of
her elaborate hairdo. Opening the wardrobe door, she
hung the dress up.

The door was a temporary shield from Tyson. Behind
it she removed her tights and her pretty underwear and
dragged the pins from her hair so it fell about her waist.
Covering of a sort, she thought, shivering, and heard
the bedsprings squeak as Tyson got into bed.

She could not cower behind the door forever. Ducking
her head, she ran for the bed and dived under the sheets,
keeping well to her side of the bed. Tyson said huskily,
'Come here, Roslin,' and reached out for her, pulling
her close. 'You're cold!' he exclaimed, and wrapped his
arms around her.

With a shock of surprise she felt the naked length of
his body along her own; he was, unlike her, very warm.
Instinctively she snuggled into him, felt his arms tighten
and heard him say, 'Look at me.'

Obediently she looked up, her features delineated by
the flickering light of the candle. He took a handful of
her hair in his fist, resting his cheek on its silken sheen,
inhaling its fragrance; then he moved back from her,
drawing the shining black strands over her breasts.

The expression on his face made her heartbeat quicken,
for in it was wonderment and all the passion she could
have wished for. Then, bending his head, he kissed the
swell of her flesh through her hair, and the agonising
sweetness of his lips on her breast made her fears seem

ridiculous. Infinitesimally she relaxed in his arms, allowing herself to enjoy the weight of his thigh over hers, the roughness of his body hair against her belly, the smooth slide of his muscles and the masculine tang of his skin. It was new and exciting; but more than that, it was Tyson, whom she loved.

Her breasts felt heavy with desire, their tips aching for his touch; her fingers caressed his thick, dark hair, his nape, the flat planes of his back, digging into the taut muscles. As his tongue encompassed her nipple, she cried out his name in sudden ecstasy, and as if this had been a signal to take her by storm he began raining kisses on her, her face, her mouth, her breasts, until any residual fear was drowned in the immensity of her longing for him.

His hands slid lower, discovering the curve of her waist and the soft skin of her thighs, moulding her to him, so that she felt all the power of his arousal. For a moment fear returned, for this was indeed the unknown. But he was assailing her with his mouth and hands, his fingers seeking out the secret places of her body, playing her as if she were a musical instrument from which he would extract rhythm and colour and beauty, and she was helpless to resist him. Deep inside, she felt the trembling begin again. Her hips moved against him with untaught, primitive fierceness; she ached to have him within her where he would claim her as his own. Where he belonged.

She drew her breath in sharply as he entered her. His eyes, turbulent with the pride of the conqueror, held her own until she was drowning in their stormy grey depths even as her body was drowning in the rhythms within her. She could hear someone panting. His back was slicked with sweat. Then she was seized by a throbbing she could not control, that arched her body into his so that she clutched him as if she were indeed drowning. The pulse of his own release joined hers in a crescendo unlike any she had ever known, that overwhelmed her in its intensity.

Her face seemed to be buried in his chest, and the panting breaths had been her own; the pounding against her cheek was the pounding of his heart. Decrescendo...

I'm different, Roslin thought dazedly. I belong to Tyson now.

In the quiet that followed the storm she wanted to say, I love you, for what words could be more natural in the intimacy of their embrace? Yet the words would not come. She lay still, wondering why they should seem so impossible. Because Tyson had taken her so fast, in such intense silence? Because, although he had not hurt her, his frantic lovemaking had somehow not allowed for subtlety or tenderness?

Or was she, so inexperienced, being too harsh a judge? Would the second time be different?

She stole a glance at him through her lashes. His eyes were shut, his breathing still hoarse in his throat, and she knew she lacked the courage to say those three small words that were so fraught with meaning. It was a meaning he did not want, she thought, in an unwelcome return of fear. He had taken her the only way he knew, for tenderness was not in his nature. Nor, more frighteningly, was love.

Suddenly she could bear the silence no longer. 'Tyson?' she whispered. 'Are you all right?'

He nodded, opening his eyes. They were filled with such anguish and confusion that Roslin took his face in her hands and said strongly, 'What's wrong? Was I a— a disappointment to you?'

His lips smiled at her, although his eyes did not change. 'Of course not. You were as beautiful as I've always known you would be.'

'Then what is it?'

So quickly that she was startled, he rolled off her. 'I'm the one who should be asking the questions, Roslin, not you.' The grey eyes impaled her. 'What about you? Were you happy with what happened in this bed—totally and unreservedly happy?'

Roslin had never learned to lie. She said, fumbling for words, 'It was the first time, Tyson...practice makes perfect, I'm sure.'

He said with cruel insight, 'You would have preferred the trappings of romance, Roslin. Endearments. Gentle caresses. Soft words of love whispered into your ear. Admit that I'm right!'

She hugged her arms across her breast. 'Those would come with time,' she whispered.

'Would they?' He gave a humourless bark of laughter. 'I'm not so sure. I've never said the words "I love you" to a single living soul—do you think that I'm likely to start now?'

'Yes! If you give yourself a chance.'

'I can't change—it's too late.'

'Then you'll never be free,' she cried.

'Where are my car keys, Roslin?'

A hand seemed to have clenched itself around her heart. She faltered, 'You're not leaving?'

'I shouldn't have made love to you, it was wrong of me and I'm sorry. But at least I can have the decency to get out now before I do any more damage.' In one swift movement Tyson rolled over to the other side of the bed. Then he stood up and walked to the chair where he had put his clothes.

He was lean-flanked and very beautiful; and more remote from her than she would have believed possible. Roslin said in a voice she scarcely recognised as her own, 'When will you come back?'

He drew his trousers on and fastened them before answering her. 'I made a mistake when I agreed to this...relationship, as you call it. I should have realised it was a pipe dream. I'll be leaving town as soon as I can...I think I have a buyer for the house.'

'So we're back where we were a month ago,' she said blankly. 'Tyson, you can't just disappear.'

'If you'll tell me where you hid my keys, I can.'

Her trick with the keys now seemed utter foolishness, a silly, childish prank for which she was being horribly punished. 'They're in the cupboard to the left of the sink, behind the vegetable oil,' she said, adding with unconscious pathos, 'Please don't go!'

After cramming his shirt into his waistband, Tyson picked up his shoes and jacket. Not until then did he look at her. She was clutching the sheet to her breast, her hair tangled, her face ravaged. He said hoarsely, 'Don't you understand, Roslin—you deserve someone better than me? Someone normal who can give you the kind of love you were surrounded with as a child. All I would do is disappoint you, over and over again. I won't do that to you!'

In a small clear voice Roslin said, 'Don't I have any choice in the matter?'

His muttered expletive brought a flush of anger to her cheeks. 'You're a coward, Tyson McCully! You're running away because you're afraid to stand and fight. You could fight Bradleigh in the schoolyard, but you won't fight me because I'm asking you to change, to grow, to throw off the lessons of your childhood rather than let them dictate the way you live——'

'I'd be a coward if I stayed. I won't risk hurting you!'

'You *are* hurting me! You hurt me the last time you left here forever, which was exactly four weeks ago, and now you're hurting me again.' She sat up, tossing back her hair, too distraught to bother covering herself. 'I can't stand this emotional seesaw, on one day, off the next. If you leave here now, it really is goodbye. Don't come back—ever!'

Her features were fined to the essentials by a rage that was nine parts pain; her breasts seemed to shimmer in the glow of candlelight. Tyson, looking like a man on a rack, grated, 'I won't. Roslin, what I'm doing is for the best!'

She had no reply for that. She watched him blunder from the room with none of his usual grace, heard, like a death knell, the creaking of the fourth and seventh steps, and after a short silence the slam of the front door. She got up and walked, naked, into the spare room, whose windows overlooked the front of the house. The lights of the van leaped on, intensifying the blackness of the night. The van drove away.

She went back to bed, and for the rest of the night lay dry-eyed in the darkness.

The summer days slowly passed. Roslin had the piano tuned, wrote to the three schools with the highest reputations in the field of composition, including Juilliard, and cancelled the contractors who were to have fixed the roof. Instead she called a lawyer in Bath, which was in the opposite direction to Buckton, and arranged to have all the documents drawn up so she could donate Great-Aunt Mellicent's inheritance to the bird society. Amy and Annabel would be pleased—as, she supposed, would the birds.

She planned to stay on the property until the end of August; then she would go back to Boston. Sadder, she often thought, but not necessarily wiser. Unless she counted the learning of that hard lesson that one cannot change another person against his wishes.

She did not see Tyson on her rare trips into Carmel, nor did she hear from him. A week after his departure from her bed and her life, she went to see Amy and Annabel, a visit she had delayed because she had been afraid of losing her composure in the face of their innocent questions. They were sitting in the wicker rocking-chairs on Amy's porch, and sprang to their feet, twittering like songbirds, when they saw her coming.

'How nice, dear. I was just saying to Annabel that we hadn't seen you for a while.'

'Lean your bicycle against the fence, that's right.'

'Do come in out of the sun.'

'Lemonade, dear?'

'An old recipe of my mother's.'

'How are you?'

And, coyly from Amy, the question Roslin had been steeling herself for, 'How's Tyson, dear?'

'We haven't seen him lately, have we, Amy?'

'Not for a week or so.'

'We heard his house had sold.'

'He's to vacate at the end of August.'

They paused, bright-eyed, Amy with the lemonade pitcher poised over a glass, Annabel holding a plate of tiny cookies. Roslin said with a touch of desperation, 'We're not seeing each other any more.'

'Again?' squeaked Amy as she poured the lemonade.

'You said that once before,' Annabel reminded her.

Roslin took a cookie. 'I know. But this time it's final.'

'Absolutely final?' Annabel said sternly.

'Over forever?' asked the more romantic Amy.

Roslin took a swallow of the lemonade, blinked at its tartness, and said, 'Yes.'

Amy's faded blue eyes filled with tears. 'I was going to wear my new hat to the wedding,' she quavered. 'It has bluebirds on it.'

'What happened?' said Annabel.

'He's afraid of love.' Roslin took another gulp of the lemonade, wishing she could banish the vision of herself walking up the aisle to meet Tyson, Amy and the bluebirds cheering her on. She would have had to wear off-white for the less-than-virginal, she thought, with a pang of the crippling agony that could seize her at any time of the day or night.

Perhaps something showed in her face. Annabel said, 'Is there anything we can do to help?' while Amy added, sounding as tart as any lemon,

'The man's a fool.'

For Amy those were strong words. Roslin said, 'He's convinced he's acting for the best. Saving me pain in the long run.'

'I'd like to knock some sense into him,' Amy announced, brandishing her glass as if it were a truncheon.

Roslin said firmly, 'You mustn't do anything of the sort. In fact, you mustn't do or say anything at all. No one else can change Tyson—he can only do it himself.'

'She's right, Amy,' said Annabel.

'But it seems so sad,' Amy wailed.

This time it was Roslin's eyes that filled with tears, although tragic was the word she would have used in preference to sad. Hastily she buried her nose in her glass.

'Presumably Tyson will leave at the end of the month. What will you do, dear?' Annabel asked.

'I'll go back to Boston,' Roslin said overloudly.

'We'll miss you,' Amy and Annabel said in chorus.

Roslin knew she could not take much more of this. Although she had not planned to tell them yet, she said, 'I'm having the documents drawn up to give the property to the bird society.'

'Oh!' Amy gasped. 'Oh! How wonderful!'

'So the marsh won't have to be filled in,' Annabel exclaimed. 'Mellicent would be so happy.'

'The Virginia rails will still be able to nest there.'

'So will the bitterns.'

Roslin said hurriedly, 'But you won't mention this to anyone, will you? It will be a week or so before I sign the papers.'

'Of course not,' Annabel said.

'Naturally not,' Amy echoed, pink-cheeked with pleasure. 'This calls for some elderberry wine.' But, as she got up from her chair, she added delicately, 'Please don't misunderstand us, dear—we would both have preferred you and Tyson to be living at Mellicent's. But if that's not to be, then you've made a wonderful decision.'

'Extremely generous,' Annabel added.

'Beneficent!' Amy pronounced, and went for the wine.

When Roslin pedalled home an hour later, she felt more cheerful, either from the company or the wine or a combination of both. But the next day the weather changed from sunshine to rain, the roof began to leak again, and she could not get out in the garden and take

out her frustration and unhappiness on the lawnmower
and the weeds. She played the piano a great deal and on
the third day of rain decided the roof could leak all it
liked, she was going to Boston to get some of her music
books.

The decision made her feel better immediately. So
much better that she wondered if she would come back.
What was she trying to prove by staying in a lonely old
house that leaked like a sieve?

The answer flashed into her brain as if supplied by a
computer. She was staying because against all the odds
she was still hoping Tyson would change his mind.

Damn him, she raged, then phoned the bus company
for the timetable and went upstairs to pack an overnight
bag. The local bus that made connections with the inter-
state bus stopped at the little shelter at the far end of
Carmel in just over two hours; she would take a taxi
into town.

She was almost ready to leave when she remembered
the dogs. Blackie was still insisting on his freedom, so
she could leave food under the tree for him; but she could
not leave the dogs alone. Nor could she expect Amy and
Annabel to feed them. She would have to take them with
her. Another phone call to the bus company established
that for a rather exorbitant fee they would supply trav-
elling cages. Jeff will love that, Roslin thought, and went
to find their leashes.

It was still raining when she got to the shelter, whose
occupants, also waiting for the bus, included a small girl
with blonde curls who was terrified of dogs. Roslin
therefore waited on the pavement in the rain, Mutt
barking at every passing car, Jeff sitting with his head
drooping in a way calculated to instil maximum guilt.

Mutt had just succeeded in winding the leash several
times around Roslin's ankles, getting her very wet in the
process, when a grey camper that Roslin would have recognised anywhere rolled up to the kerb and Tyson

jumped out. He came round the front of the van and demanded without preliminaries, 'Are you leaving?'

He had lost weight, Roslin thought numbly. And he was as white about the mouth as he had been the night of the prowler. 'I'm going to Boston,' she said shortly. 'Stop it, Mutt!'

'For good?'

Mutt's tail was flailing her calves as he struggled to lick Tyson's hand. Traitor, she thought, trying to uncoil the leash and nearly overbalancing as she did so.

Tyson rapped, 'Down, Mutt!' Mutt sat down, gazing adoringly at him. Even Jeff's tail swished across the wet pavement. .

'For good?' Tyson repeated, his eyes like chips of granite.

Very conscious of the half-dozen people waiting in the shelter, equally conscious that she was making another unwise decision, Roslin said, 'I'm going to get some music. I'll be back Wednesday evening.' Wednesday was three days from now. 'Why do you care?' she asked recklessly.

He did not answer. 'Are you taking the dogs because you can't bear to be parted from them, or because you couldn't find anyone to look after them?'

'The latter.'

'Give them to me. I'll stay at the house and take care of them.'

Her jaw dropped. Then, over the hiss of tyres on the road and the patter of the rain, she heard the deeper growl of the approaching bus. 'Forever lasted ten days this time,' she said furiously.

He gave her the full benefit of his smile. 'Look upon it as a favour for a friend,' he said. 'Particularly if it involves feeding the cat. You'll have to give me the key to the house.'

'We're not friends!'

'Goodness knows what we are.' The bus-driver blasted his horn at Tyson, for the camper was parked in his slot. Tyson ignored him. 'The key, Roslin.'

With an ostentatious grinding of gears, the bus pulled around the camper. Mutt leaped to attack it, jerking Roslin against Tyson's chest. His arms went around her as her cheek slapped into his wet yellow slicker. She struggled frantically, overwhelmed by memories that she could not bear. Tyson yelled at Mutt, who sat down in the ditch, and the people in the shelter began filing on to the bus. 'I've got to go,' she gasped. 'Let go, Tyson!'

'The key.'

He was unwinding the leash from her legs; she looked down at his bent head, the hair rain-damp, and with an immense physical effort did not touch him. Scrabbling in her bag, she produced the house key. ''Here,' she said baldly.

He straightened, putting the key carefully in his pocket, then taking the leashes from her hand. Even the brush of his thumb against her flesh was so familiar that she almost cried out. He said, 'You'd better get on board. I'll see you on Wednesday.'

Glancing over her shoulder, Roslin saw that everyone else was on the bus. She looked up at him, her heartbeat almost suffocating her, and said breathlessly, 'I love you, Tyson McCully.' Then she ran for the bus.

The driver snapped the door shut behind her, took her fare, and the bus lurched away from the kerb. The windows were steamed over; all she could see was the yellow blur of Tyson's slicker and then the grey of the empty pavement. Staggering as the bus gained momentum, she found a seat near the back, leaned her head back and closed her eyes.

Two unwise decisions in five minutes, she thought. You excelled yourself there, Roslin.

But her mood of self-castigation could not last. All she could think of as the bus trundled towards the main road where she would catch the connection to Boston was that Tyson would be waiting for her when she got home.

CHAPTER TWELVE

MRS GRANMONT, stout, her black hair owing more to
artifice than to nature, had been the housekeeper at the
Hebbs' for as long as Roslin could remember. Roslin
had phoned ahead, because the bus got in late at night;
Mrs Granmont, in consequence, was expecting her.
'Come in, Roslin, come in. What have you been doing,
starving yourself up there in the wilderness?'

The wilderness, to Mrs Granmont, was anywhere
outside the city limits. Roslin hugged her and said af-
fectionately, 'You've been making doughnuts, haven't
you?'

'Just as well—put a little flesh on your bones.'

Roslin said carefully, 'Where's my uncle? Has he gone
to bed?'

'He's in New York. Since last week,' the housekeeper
said with a twinkle in her eye; Roslin had sensed long
ago that no love was lost between Mrs Granmont and
Colby. 'Your room's all ready and I'll make a nice cup
of tea,' she added, and bustled to the kitchen.

Roslin's bedroom looked exactly as it had when she
had left, and when she went down the hall to the studio
the gleaming Steinway seemed to greet her as an old
friend rather than the enemy it had almost become. Her
mother's cello stood in the corner; there were fresh
flowers on the table. She was home...and downstairs
Mrs Granmont was waiting for her with some of the
doughnuts that had been her favourites since she was a
little girl.

When Roslin boarded the bus on Wednesday to go
back to Maine she was feeling rested in body and soul.
In the quiet of the studio she had worked on the melody
that had come to her on the beach after her first meeting

with Tyson, the hours passing like minutes, each one confirming in her that she had made the right decision for her future. And somehow those hours of work in a room redolent with memories had instilled in her an optimism for her personal future. Surely even Tyson would now recognise the cords that bound him to her, and understand that these recurring reunions were more significant than the separations he kept insisting on.

She would be seeing him that very evening. And he now knew that she loved him....

However, half an hour after they had crossed the border into New Hampshire a truck pulled out of a side road directly in front of the bus; the bus, unable to stop in time, drove the truck into a telephone pole, and after a nightmare interlude of police cars and ambulances Roslin and her fellow travellers were told that the driver of the truck was not seriously injured but the bus was badly enough damaged that a replacement would have to come from Boston. There would be a delay.

Although Roslin tried twice to phone Tyson, the line seemed to be out of order. As she and the other passengers waited on board the bus, the police brought hot coffee and, ironically, doughnuts; Roslin ate a doughnut, which was not nearly as good as Mrs Granmont's, declined the coffee, and tried to sleep. She did not want to see this delay as a bad omen.

The replacement bus arrived in the small hours of the morning. Roslin got off at the turn-off to Carmel, engaged a taxi because she was both too impatient and too tired to wait for the local bus, and at nine o'clock was winding along the narrow road to Great-Aunt Mellicent's.

She smelled the smoke before she saw it. An acrid reek of burning overlaid the tang of the sea and the homely woodland scents of trees and wildflowers. Suddenly frightened, she said to the driver, 'Hurry—I think there's something wrong,' and rolled down her window.

As they climbed the last rise by the marsh she could see the smoke, blue-grey against the deeper blue of the

sky, hanging over the trees that encircled the house. Her
breath caught in her throat as explanations tumbled
through her brain. Tyson was burning brush. The woods
behind the house were on fire. The garden shed had
burned.

But there was too much smoke: a pall that had settled
on the crowns of the old oak trees, and had wreathed
the elms like an Elizabethan ruff. Clutching the back of
the driver's seat, Roslin craned her neck as the taxi
climbed the driveway. She saw the fire engines first because they were red, a garish red against the trees. Then
she saw the house.

It had been reduced to a heap of smouldering beams,
some upright like blackened tree trunks after a forest
fire, some angled where they had fallen. The roof was
gone. The doors, the windows, the rooms themselves
were gone. Only the fireplace stood in splendid isolation
among the ruins. The fireplace and, parked under the
maples at the far end of the driveway, Tyson's van.

Roslin flung herself out of the taxi. A group of firemen
was poking desultorily among the charred timbers; two
more, clad in black hip boots and heavy yellow jackets,
were standing beside one of the trucks. They watched
her stumble across the gravel towards them.

She grabbed the nearer man by the sleeve. He had
grey eyes, she saw, although not as grey as Tyson's. Her
voice strangled by terror, she croaked, 'Tyson—he was
in the house...'

She was swaying on her feet, her complexion white as
ashes. The fireman put an arm around her before she
could fall and said strongly, 'There was no one in the
house.'

Her eyes glazed, she was pounding him on the chest.
'He was sleeping in the house—don't you understand?'

The other man, older, deeper-voiced, said bluntly,
'We've gone through the wreckage from one end to the
other. There was no one sleeping in that house, ma'am,
I can assure you.'

She looked at him blindly. 'I—are you *sure*?'

'Yes, ma'am, I'm sure.'

His face was streaked with soot and lined with tiredness, but he also looked kind. Feeling her head begin to spin, Roslin cried, 'Then where *is* he?'

'Can't tell you that, ma'am.'

For a moment she leaned her forehead on his jacket, remembering the wetness of Tyson's yellow slicker against her skin at the bus shelter and the way she had blurted, 'I love you.' Then her conscious mind took in the noise that subconsciously she must have been aware of for some time: the frantic barking of two dogs, one high-pitched and as hysterical as she felt, the other a mournful baying. 'The dogs,' she gasped, 'where are they?'

'Someone had tied them to the tree beyond the van. Out of reach of the flames.'

She shivered. 'I don't understand.'

'This is—was—your house?'

The younger fireman had spoken. 'Yes,' Roslin muttered. 'I was away for three days, and my friend Tyson was staying here and taking care of the dogs for me...' Her brain fumbled for facts. 'When would the fire have started?'

'We got the call at three a.m. It was well under way by then.'

Behind her the taxi driver was pressing on the horn. She said faintly, 'I'd better pay him,' and, turning her back on the ugly ruin of Great-Aunt Mellicent's house, she walked across the gravel towards the car. Her overnight bag was sitting on the ground, and it was plain the cab driver did not want to get involved with the scene in front of him. After she had thrust a bill into his outstretched hand, he drove away. Then she walked over to the van and opened the driver's door.

The keys were in the ignition. Tyson's slicker was lying on the passenger's seat, along with a paperback with a bookmark a third of the way through the pages.

As she closed the door and approached the dogs, Mutt almost bowling her over in his enthusiasm, Jeff soberly wagging his tail, she saw they had been tied to the trunk of the maple with brand-new nylon twine. Their water dish was lying on the ground.

'What happened, Mutt?' she said. 'Where's Tyson?'

Mutt slobbered all over her hand while Jeff leaned his nose on her knee; Blackie scowled at her from the shrubbery. She stroked Jeff's soft, drooping ears and tried to think.

Tyson had not been in the house when it burned to the ground. Someone had moved the van. Someone had tied the dogs up.

Tyson?

If so, why? If not, where was he?

She could not answer either question. But she was going to find out the answers. She strode back to the house and said to the older fireman, 'Thank you for keeping the fire from the woods, it would have been dreadful if they had caught—the house was old, and I suppose, in one way, no great loss. I'm going into town now to see if I can locate my friend. I hope I wasn't rude to you when I arrived . . . I—I was upset.'

'No problem, ma'am. Hope you find him.'

Roslin went back to the van and drove into Carmel, to Tyson's house. He did not answer the door; not that she had really expected him to. Her stomach churning with mingled fury and fear, she drove to Buckton.

The secretary in Bradleigh Waldron's office was beautifully dressed, making Roslin aware of how crumpled and untidy she must look after a night on the bus and the shock of the fire. This realisation did nothing to cool her anger. On the way to Buckton she had given thought to her strategy, which could range from weeping and pleading to attacking from strength; she knew now she would follow the second course, even though it was basically dishonest. She said, 'Is Mr Waldron in, please?'

'May I tell him who's calling?'

'No,' said Roslin. 'I'll announce myself.' She marched across the plush carpet, pulled the door open and slammed it shut behind her.

Bradleigh Waldron was seated behind his fortress-like desk. When he saw her, the tiniest trace of emotion crossed his face. For Roslin it was enough. She leaned over the desk and said in a voice as cutting as the blade of her Italian knife, 'Where's Tyson?'

Bradleigh made a steeple out of his fingers. The number of diamonds seemed to have increased, Roslin noticed with a further flare of rage.

Rather than answering her question, he countered, 'Ready to put your property on the market, Miss Hebb?'

'It's too late for that, Mr Waldron.'

As his hands twitched, the diamonds sparkled and flashed. 'What do you mean?'

Mentally crossing her fingers against the lie, she replied, 'I've deeded the entire property to the bird society. The papers were signed before I went to Boston.'

His double chins quivered. 'I'm not a fool! That place is worth a cool half-million—you wouldn't just give it away.'

'I already have.' Roslin gave him a mocking smile. 'You shouldn't judge everyone by your standards, Mr Waldron.' Then she leaned forward again, remembering the pall of smoke and those terror-filled moments when she thought Tyson had perished in the flames. 'Where's Tyson?' she repeated.

Although she could tell he had been shaken by her news, he sneered, 'How should I know?'

'You know. And you're going to tell me, or else I'll go to the nearest phone and call the police.' She straightened, playing her second, quite imaginary card. 'You should pick your kidnappers with more care. One of them left four very clear footprints in the ground at the base of the tree where he tied the dogs. It shouldn't be difficult to trace the owner of those footprints, and less difficult to connect him with you.'

'You're lying!'

She was. She said coldly, 'Let's bargain, Mr Waldron. You tell me where Tyson is, and I won't lay charges. Otherwise I'll go to the police. Arson is a criminal offence. As is kidnapping.' And she tilted her chin with a quite spurious air of confidence.

It must have convinced Bradleigh. He said viciously, 'All right, all right—you win this round.'

'I've won them all, Mr Waldron. Because if there is ever the slightest bit of trouble regarding that property, I'll produce the photographs of the footprints and I'll hound you through every court in the land.'

Looking as though he would like to throttle her, Bradleigh spat, 'Drive three miles west out of Buckton. Take the first dirt road after the church, go half a mile and you'll come to a barn. Your friend Tyson is in there.' He finished venomously, 'I told 'em to tie him up good and tight.'

The schoolyard, Roslin thought sickly, was not so very far away. Without saying a word she stalked across the carpet and left the building. She felt soiled, unclean, as though she had been in contact with something loathsome.

She drove west out of Buckton, taking careful note of the mileage. An austere white church shaded a graveyard three miles out of town, and a quarter of a mile beyond it was an unmarked dirt road to the left. She turned down it.

It was a pretty little road, flanked with fields of grain and lined by maple and birch trees that cast a dappled pattern of sun and shadow on the grass. But Roslin was frightened again, and in no mood for the beauties of nature. What if Tyson was hurt? Worse, what if he was not here at all? Then what would she do?

The barn was new, solidly constructed out of clapboard shingles; the lower floor, she saw with a sinking heart, had no windows at all, and the big double doors where chained and padlocked. For the first time it occurred to her that she might not be able to rescue Tyson, that she would have been more sensible to have brought a hacksaw and a ladder. Even a strong man or two. She parked the van and climbed out, standing by the open door.

Somewhere in the woods a bird was calling, two notes over and over again with monotonous regularity. The air was very still, not even the leaves moving, and further to the west thunderclouds were piling in the sky. She did not have to worry about the roof leaking in Great-Aunt Mellicent's house, Roslin thought foolishly. She no longer had a roof.

She wanted to call out Tyson's name, but something in the stillness of the clearing paralysed her throat muscles. Then she heard, from the back of the barn, a scraping noise.

Bradleigh had capitulated too easily, she thought, her feet rooted to the ground. His hired helpers were still here. This was a trap, and she had walked into it as meekly as a lamb to the slaughter.

She climbed in the van again, squeezed between the seats, and lifted the rear seat as if she were going to fold out the bed; from the storage space underneath she extracted the long metal jack. Thus armed, she crept around the barn to the back.

The front of the barn was two storeyed. The back had, jutting out from it, a steep-roofed section only one storey high, that at its farthest point from the barn was overhung by a huge oak tree. The scraping noise she had heard was Tyson inching along the ridgepole towards the tree. He was crouched over, gripping the rooftree with both hands. He was wearing jeans and a checked shirt.

The jack slipped from her nerveless fingers. She had not fainted yet, Roslin thought dizzily, she must not start now.

Then Tyson looked up, perhaps alerted by the thud as the jack hit the ground. He must have seen her instantly: a slim figure in a flowered shirt and blouse standing in the sunlit clearing, her hands limp at her sides. He tried to stand up, almost lost his balance, and half fell back on the roof, clutching the ridge again. 'Roslin?' he croaked. *'Roslin?'*

'It's me,' she said.

'I—are you all right?'

'Yes.'

He rested his head on his sleeve, his shoulders bowed. Then Roslin gave a cry of alarm as he lost his grip, sliding a couple of feet down the steep angle of the roof before he could stop himself. She watched, helplessly, as he crawled up again, and began his tortured progress towards the tree.

It seemed to take forever. Then she had to watch, willing him not to fall, while he flung himself from the roof into the limbs of the tree, wrapping his arms and legs around a branch, grunting with effort as he lunged for the trunk. It was a feat worthy of Tarzan; she did not, however, find it amusing.

He could find footholds now, swinging himself towards the ground. The lowest limb of the tree was perhaps fifteen feet above the grass; Roslin remembered the rescue of Blackie, and would have given anything to have had the ladder now. Tyson looked over his shoulder, pushed himself away from the trunk, and fell to the ground, his body curled in self-protection. She ran towards him.

The breath had been knocked from his lungs. Kneeling beside him, she put her hand on his shoulder, felt the bunch of muscle and heard him gasp for air, and knew he was real. She closed her eyes, her whole being a vast prayer of thanksgiving.

Then Tyson rolled over and pulled her to her feet. Gripping her forearms as hard as he had gripped the rooftree, he said raggedly, 'Roslin, I love you. I love you, I need you, I want to be with you always—will you marry me?'

Wondering if she was dreaming, she gaped up at him. He looked terrible, his face drained of colour except for a bruise over one eye which was a lurid mixture of yellow, pink and purple. 'You're delirious,' she said.

'No, I'm not—I've come to my senses. You told me you love me…didn't you mean it?'

'Oh, yes. I meant it. But do you?'

'I've never understood anything more clearly in my life than the fact that I love you. I was a fool, Roslin, a damned fool.'

There was such strained desperation in his face that she was beginning to believe him. Besides, he was swearing again. She said with an incredulous smile, 'Tyson, are you really saying you love me?'

The humour that she seemed always to have known gleamed in his eyes. 'That's what I'm trying to tell you.'

'You *need* me?'

'That, too.'

Her smile was illuminating her whole face. 'I can't believe this is happening!'

He said roughly, 'I don't blame you. It took last night to bring me to my senses—I've been so worried about you, I nearly went out of my mind when I came to in that bloody barn and thought of you arriving home to that bunch of thugs...' His face convulsed.

'Tyson,' she said, 'darling Tyson, you look awful. You're going to fall down if you don't lie down. Let's go to the van and I'll put some cold water on that bruise and make you some coffee.'

If anything, his grip tightened. 'Tell me first that you love me,' he said hoarsely.

She said with all the intensity she was capable of, 'I love you more than I can say...with heart and mind and soul. I love you today, I'll love you tomorrow, I'll love you forever.'

There was a small silence. Then Tyson said with a crooked smile, 'You always were generous.' Dropping his head to her shoulder, leaning his weight on her so that she staggered, he added, 'They didn't hurt you?'

'They weren't there. We'll exchange stories in the van, come along,' she said firmly, putting an arm around his waist and steering him towards the front of the barn.

She had parked the van in the shade. After they climbed in through the side door, Tyson lifted the roof section by the metal bars while Roslin busied herself at the sink. She turned to ask him something and saw, as he clicked the catch in place, the bracelets of reddened flesh around his wrists, encrusted with patches of dried blood. Horrified, she said, 'What happened?'

He looked uncomfortable. 'They tied me up,' he said briefly. 'They weren't very professional, but it still took a while to get free.'

She went to him as an arrow to the gold, buried her face in his chest and held on to him as tightly as she could. He said gently, 'It's OK, Roslin, it looks a lot worse than it is.'

'They were h-horrible... Tyson, I do love you.'

He hugged her, his damaged wrists not impairing his strength, and said, 'I love you, too... we're starting to sound like a cracked record.'

She looked up at him. 'You're sure you're not just admitting all this because you feel like the wrath of God and you've been through an awful night, and tomorrow you'll wish you hadn't?'

'You take a lot of convincing, honeybunch.'

There was such tenderness in his voice that it was an effort for her to frown. 'Of course I do... look at the chase you led me, saying goodbye forever every second day.'

'I promise never to do that again.'

'Will you put it in writing?'

'What a shrew you are,' he remarked. 'I have a better idea—let's go to bed and I'll try and convince you there that I'm a changed man.'

'Here? In the van?'

'Fewer mosquitoes. And no one will be coming down this road, it belongs to Bradleigh.'

She gave him her most dazzling smile. 'OK,' she said.

Kissing the tip of her nose, Tyson said, 'That's your sea-witch smile—works every time.' He set to work flattening the rear seat while Roslin produced sheets and pillows, and between them they made up the bed. Then Tyson said huskily, 'I want to undress you this time, Roslin.'

She was standing in the brightness of midday rather than the glow of candlelight; but there was in Tyson's face a new gentleness, almost a humility, that told her that he, too, was treading new ground. 'If you'll allow me to do the same,' she said softly.

'There's nothing I'd like better.'

Their clothes were removed in a trembling silence, broken only by the twittering of the birds in the trees. Then they lay on the bed, and Tyson began caressing her, slowly, as if he had all the time in the world to show her how much he loved her. As he explored the smooth curves of her body he spoke to her of his love, encouraging her to match him, caress for caress, pleasure for pleasure, until their murmurs of delight drifted into the sunlit air. It was a lovemaking as different in quality from the first as day from night, for it was suffused by that sunlight, by a love that could be openly enjoyed and joyfully expressed. Yet, like the first time, it ended in a storm of passion that shook Roslin to the roots of her being.

She found she was clinging to him, at one and the same time glorying in his weight and shaken by a spasm of weeping. Tyson eased her on her side, kissing the tears from her face. 'What is it, sweetheart, what's wrong?'

She knew him very well. 'Nothing,' she sobbed. 'That was the most beautiful experience of my life. But, Tyson, when I got home this morning I thought you were dead...that we would never have this second chance to love each other... We're so l-lucky.'

Stroking his hair, she told him about her disrupted bus journey and about the blackened ruins of the house, and the telling calmed her, so that by the time she came to her interview with Bradleigh she was able to relate it with gusto. 'So he won't be bothering us again,' she finished triumphantly.

'And why were you carrying the jack when you came round the corner of the barn?'

'I thought the men were still here.'

Although he was laughing, there was a spark in Tyson's eyes. 'You're as brave as a lion,' he said.

'I was scared out of my wits,' she confessed.

'That's what bravery is.' He kissed her very thoroughly.

Pink-cheeked, Roslin murmured, 'We seem to be improving at a quite astonishing rate.'

'Try this one.'

Minutes later she emerged, giggling. 'Enough! Now it's your turn, Tyson. What happened to you last night?'

He grinned at her ruefully. 'You sure you want to hear this? It's not such a glorious story as yours.'

Despite the bruise, he looked so young and carefree that she was struck again by the wonder of her love for him. 'So those impassioned kisses were just meant to distract me?' she said.

He raised one brow. 'You weren't even the tiniest bit distracted?'

'A truthful answer to that question would inflate your ego. Tell me what happened, Tyson.'

'About nine-thirty last night the dogs started barking. I thought it was you, so I went outside. Whereupon three of them set on me. I did my fair share of damage, but they had a pad soaked with what I suppose was chloroform, and half-way through the fight I went out like a light.' He grimaced. 'They had masks on, like the prowler you described, so I can't even identify them. Anyway, I came to in the barn, nearly went crazy wondering what they were doing to you—which is when I realised how much I both loved and needed you—eventually got out of the ropes, climbed to the second floor, squeezed through a window and ended up on the roof.' He nuzzled into her neck. 'After which I was seduced by a beautiful young maiden.'

'You did your fair share of the seducing,' she rejoined, resting her cheek on his hair. Then, with an exquisite care, she stroked one of his wrists. 'You freed yourself from more than the ropes last night, Tyson.'

His voice muffled, he said, 'But what about *your* freedom, Roslin? Will you lose it by marrying me?'

With deep conviction she said, 'With you I can be myself—that's the greatest freedom there is.'

He raised his head. 'I'll do my best to love you the way you should be loved. I'll try not to shut you out, not to hide my own needs and vulnerabilities...but it's all new to me, and I may not always succeed.'

She said strongly, 'We have the rest of our lives to learn.'

'I love you,' Tyson said. Then a smile chased across his face. 'And I'm sure if I fall short, you'll let me know.'

Roslin drew a finger down his chest. 'I'm starting to learn the ways to gain your attention,' she said demurely.

He captured her hand. 'We could live in New York and you could go to Juilliard. We could live anywhere, for that matter—anywhere except Carmel.'

'No Carmel,' she concurred. 'But after New York could we live in the country? And have a garden like Great-Aunt Mellicent's?'

'Once we have children, I think we should.'

Roslin gave a breathless laugh. 'You really do want to marry me?'

'It's all a plot, Roslin—to give me a built-in concert pianist,' he teased. 'Yes, I want to marry you.'

'We'll have to invite Amy and Annabel to the wedding. Amy has a new hat, with bluebirds on it.'

'You know, if it hadn't been for Bradleigh and his mighty team of kidnappers, we might not have got together—do you think we should invite him to the wedding as well?'

'No,' said Roslin. 'I think that would be going too far.'

'Come here,' said Tyson, 'and I'll show you what going too far means.'

Coming Next Month

Available in August wherever paperback books are sold, or through Harlequin Reader Service:

In the U.S.
901 Fuhrmann Blvd.
P.O. Box 1397
Buffalo, N.Y. 14240-1397

In Canada
P.O. Box 603
Fort Erie, Ontario
L2A 5X3

Take 4 bestselling love stories FREE

Plus get a FREE surprise gift!

Harlequin Supperromance®

A powerful restaurant conglomerate that draws the best and brightest to its executive ranks. Now almost eighty years old, Vanessa Hamilton, the founder of Hamilton House, must choose a successor.
Who will it be?

Matt Logan: He's always been the company man, the quintessential team player. But tragedy in his daughter's life and a passionate love affair made him make some hard choices....

Paula Steele: Thoroughly accomplished, with a sharp mind, perfect breeding and looks to die for, Paula thrives on challenges and wants to have it all ...
but is this right for her?

Grady O'Connor: Working for Hamilton House was his salvation after Vietnam. The war had messed him up but good and had killed his storybook marriage. He's been given a second chance—only he doesn't know what the hell he's supposed to do with it....

Harlequin Superromance invites you to enjoy Barbara Kaye's dramatic and emotionally resonant miniseries about mature men and women making life-changing decisions. Don't miss:

- • CHOICE OF A LIFETIME—a July 1990 release.
  - • CHALLENGE OF A LIFETIME
    —a December 1990 release.
- • CHANCE OF A LIFETIME—an April 1991 release.